THE HOUSE ON THE HILL

When a young man moves into the old house next door, Kate Jackson's curiosity is piqued. However, handsome Elek Costas is suspiciously reclusive, and the two get off to a bad start when he accuses her of trespassing. Whilst Kate is dubious of Elek's claim to be the rightful owner, her boyfriend Robert has his eye on acquiring the property for himself . . . Just what is the mystery of Hillside House? Kate is determined to find out!

MIRANDA BARNES

THE HOUSE ON THE HILL

Complete and Unabridged

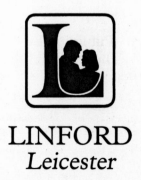

LINFORD
Leicester

First published in Great Britain in 2013

First Linford Edition
published 2015

A catalogue record for this book is available
from the British Library.

ISBN 978–1–4448–2296–0

Published by
F. A. Thorpe (Publishing)
Anstey, Leicestershire

Set by Words & Graphics Ltd.
Anstey, Leicestershire
Printed and bound in Great Britain by
T. J. International Ltd., Padstow, Cornwall

This book is printed on acid-free paper

1

She loved watching Robert when he was not aware of it. All that pent-up energy. He was on edge all the time. Constantly moving, fidgeting and analysing. He just couldn't help himself. Nothing got past him. No wonder he was so successful in business.

Just look at him now! Swaying furiously from side to side, and peering hard enough through the window to break the glass.

'Relax, Robert. Chill!' she called with amusement.

'What?'

He spun round from the kitchen window, saw her staring at him and chuckled self-consciously. 'It's just that I thought I saw a light in the old house next door.'

'Really? Are you sure?'

She got up and joined him at the window.

'I can't see it now,' he admitted, as she struggled to find what he thought he had seen. 'Perhaps I imagined it, but I don't think so.'

Hard as she stared through the encroaching darkness, she could see no light coming from Hillside House, the big, old house next door. She couldn't really see the house itself even. The light was so poor now the day was turning to night.

'Maybe there are intruders?' she said, feeling slightly apprehensive.

Robert laughed. 'After all this time? That house has been empty for years. There won't be anything left to steal by now!'

'Squatters, perhaps?'

'Out here?'

Robert laughed again, as if the idea was utterly preposterous, as indeed it probably was. The village was well off the beaten track for squatters.

'I must have imagined it,' Robert

concluded with a shrug, turning away. 'Either that or it was a trick of the light.'

Kate sat back down and let Robert fiddle with the coffee maker. He was good at that. Specialist coffee was one of his enthusiasms at the moment, especially if it involved turning on the expensive machine he had bought her for Christmas.

She had no idea herself how the thing worked. Left to her, it would still have been in its box. It was a lovely gift, she supposed. But, personally, she would rather he had spent the money on perfume. Exotic coffee wasn't one of her delights; expensive perfume was.

While the machine gurgled, with Robert poised over it, she wondered if he really had seen a light next door. Probably not. Hillside House had been empty for years, as Robert had said. There was no reason at all — no legitimate reason, at least — for anyone to be there this evening.

She yawned. 'Come and sit down,

darling! You're exhausting me just watching you.'

'Give me another minute. I've nearly got the hang of it now.'

She smiled and leant back in her chair. Gazing around the kitchen, she thought with contentment what a lovely life she led these days. This cottage. The gardening that paid for it. Robert to make coffee — when he remembered to pay her one of his visits. What more could she possibly want? Robert here full-time, perhaps? Perhaps. She wasn't sure about that. Not yet. Rather, *they* weren't sure. It hadn't been spoken of directly, but there was a tacit under-standing between them that the time was not quite right yet.

She yawned. Time would bring an answer to such questions. Possibly not a lot of time either. They had already been together for quite a while. How long was it? She frowned. She wasn't really sure. Eighteen months? A bit longer, perhaps.

'Robert, how long is it since you first

intruded into my life?'

He laughed and began to pour the coffee at last.

'Now she asks me! She knows I'm busy. She can see I'm slaving over a hot coffee machine, and she wants to know . . . Nearly two years. Why?'

She shrugged. 'Just wondered. You weren't very useful in the kitchen at first, were you?'

'Not at first, perhaps. But now look at me!'

He beamed at her. She laughed and reached up to kiss him as he leant over her.

'I should send you out into the dark to see if we have intruders next door,' she said happily, 'but I don't want to risk losing you.'

'No fear of that!'

Robert sat down. 'That old place next door is odd, though, isn't it? Do you have any idea why it's been left empty so long?'

'None at all.' She shook her head. 'I don't even know how long it's been empty. Frances just says it's been a few years. From the look of the garden — the grounds, I should say — it was very neglected long before the old gentleman who owned it passed away.'

'Army type, wasn't he?'

'I assume so. He was called Colonel Fenwick anyway. But I don't know anything about him. It was before my time here.'

Robert frowned.

'Why? What are you thinking? Come on, Robert! You've got something in mind. Tell me.'

'I was just thinking I wouldn't mind getting my hands on it. That's all.'

'You? What would you do with it? Restore the old place? That's not your usual style, is it?'

He grinned and admitted it.

'No, I would pull the old house down and replace it with half-a-dozen decent-sized detached houses. It's a huge site. There's a lot of potential there. The housing market is recovering now, as well. It would be a good time to do it.'

'Robert, don't you dare! It's a lovely old house, and I like it just the way it is. I don't want a new housing estate built right next door to me, thank you very much.

'Besides, I rather like the old garden, neglected as it is. On my little walks I always spend time thinking about how I would improve and restore it, given the chance. It's my lovely fantasy project.'

'Self-indulgence, more likely. You can't stop progress, my girl! It will happen one day, like it or not. I would just like to be the one who makes a pile of money out of the project, and provide some hard-working families with decent new homes.'

'You hypocrite! No hard-working families needing new homes would come to live here. It's too far out. You're just thinking of how you could turn a profit. We don't need new executive-style houses here.'

Robert grinned. 'You should bear in mind that they would all want their gardens doing. It would be more work for you, wouldn't it — not to mention the money you would rake in!'

'Robert, you're impossible. I give up.'

She yawned again, tired of the conversation, and tired of the day too. It had been an exhausting one. Robert was just fantasising, and she wasn't in the mood for it. He might be a property developer but his patch was the city — any city — not rural Northumberland.

Besides, they didn't even know who owned Hillside House now. So there was no-one for Robert to approach with his daft ideas and enthusiasm. Nothing was going to happen. Not for a long while, if ever. There was absolutely nothing at all for her to worry about, least of all a large-scale building site in full view from her kitchen window.

2

The next morning Kate took an early morning stroll before she started work. It was something she did regularly, even though she no longer owned a dog. The late Sandy, her Border Terrier, had been far too good a companion to replace instantly. In time, perhaps, she would have another dog, but not yet.

As usual, her route took her through the grounds of Hillside House. That particular morning nothing looked any different. Nothing had changed at all, if you ruled out the emerging blossom on the ancient apple trees that badly needed pruning and a bit of other care and attention. Robert had been mistaken, she thought with an indulgent smile. He couldn't have seen a light. He must have been tired.

She paused and swept her eyes

around the long-abandoned garden. It must have been so beautiful here in the house's heyday. Say about 1890, or thereabouts, when it was built. Goodness knows how long it had been since anyone had done any serious gardening, though. Years certainly. Decades, probably. But you could still see what the garden had once been like. It might be overgrown now, but the form and structure were still there.

The paved area on the south side of the house led via broad stone steps down to where once there had been a lawn sweeping graciously across to wide herbaceous borders, and beyond them the shrubbery. Finally, there was a belt of woodland, mostly conifers that gave the shelter from the wind that was needed at this altitude. Here, you either had the prevailing strong westerlies or you had bitter cold seeping in from the not so very distant North Sea. Neither one nor the other was good for plants and trees struggling to gain a foothold.

You could still see all that, the original shape of the garden, if you looked hard enough. But you could also see the thickets of bramble where once there had been an immaculate lawn, and you could see the birch trees and rowan that had invaded the herbaceous borders and the shrubbery. Even the steps down from the house were mossy and overgrown with ferns and bracken, all of them wild plants that had made their own way here from across the hillside. Only the southerly view across the valley, to the hills on the far side, remained unchanged. That was still lovely. No wonder the original owner had decided to build right here, on this very spot.

She resumed her stroll, thinking that it would take an awful lot of work to get rid of the gorse that had colonised large tracts of the grounds. Stunning its massed bright yellow flowers might be for months on end, but the prickly stuff was almost immortal. Chop it, pull it, burn it, and still its seedlings would appear next season, and for many years afterwards unless you took the drastic step of poisoning the ground it occupied, which to her was a no-no.

Using herbicides was an option she almost never considered in her work. They were certainly an easy way of getting rid of all the stuff you didn't want, but so much else was inevitably destroyed as well. This included all those insects and plants that had done nothing wrong, and that mostly were so very useful in maintaining the balance of nature. Birds as well. Small mammals. The whole food chain, in fact.

'Hey, you!'

She spun round, alarmed.

'What are you doing on my property?' an angry-looking young man demanded as he emerged from the woodland. 'You're trespassing. Get out now!'

She stood still, shocked, as he advanced on her.

'What do you mean?' she said, as her wits returned from wherever they had been while she day-dreamed. 'Who are you?'

'The owner of this property. Now get out — and stay out!'

'The owner? I don't think so,' she responded spiritedly. 'I don't know who you are, but you're certainly not the owner of Hillside House. I'm sure of that.

'This place has been empty for many years, and I've never seen you before. In fact, I've never seen anyone else here at all.'

'Well, now you've seen me — Elek Costas,' the man said, stabbing an index finger towards his own chest. 'I am the owner. I want you to leave now, or I will have the police remove you.'

She stared at him resolutely. 'You don't intimidate me, Mr Whatever-you-said-your-name-is. But I will leave. And when I get home, I shall call the police myself. Don't you worry!'

'Who are you?' he demanded.

'Kate Jackson. I live next door, in Fern Cottage.'

She waved in the direction of her cottage, and then set off walking back towards it, fuming. He watched her go, standing in a belligerent pose, hands on hips.

What a nerve, she thought indignantly. That man!

She was shocked, stunned, by the encounter. She had never experienced anything like it. Of one thing she was certain, though. That man had no more right to be here than she did, and probably a lot less. She was a neighbour, after all. He was not. It was outrageous of him to have spoken to her like that, whoever he was.

* * *

There was no permanent police presence in the village, of course. Not these days, and not for a long time past. The police house had stood empty ever since she had arrived in Callerton. Modern police officers preferred to own rather than rent, as one of them had told her himself. Otherwise, they couldn't get into the housing market when they retired.

As she let herself into her cottage, she was trying to remember what you had to do these days to contact them. There was an information board with instructions outside the old police house but she couldn't recall what she had once read there. So she just rang 999.

Her call was answered by a brisk woman in a far-away town who seemed to require the story of Kate's life before she would even consider dealing with the problem Kate wanted to put to her. But eventually it was done, the message conveyed.

'A trespasser in an empty property?' the woman repeated in a monotone, as if it was the most boring and ridiculous thing she had ever heard.

'Yes. That's right. It's been empty for a number of years. I live next door and I've never seen anyone there until this morning.'

'Someone will look into it,' the

woman assured her with what sounded like a heavy accompanying sigh.

That was that. The call was ended. Kate was left restless in her kitchen, wondering how long it would take for 'someone to look into it'. Hillside House could well be burnt down before anyone arrived to check on the trespasser she had met. The police needed to come here right now. Oh, it was so frustrating!

* * *

She was in no mood now to work on the garden design she was preparing for a client in the village. Sitting down at her desk and her computer was quite beyond her in the state of agitation the early-morning encounter had produced. Instead, she went out into her own garden and began a bout of strenuous digging and weeding.

That occupied her for a little while. There was nothing like hard manual work to get rid of anger and frustration, she thought breathlessly. Nothing like it at all! But she couldn't sustain the effort. She flung her spade to the ground and kicked out at a big clod of earth she had dislodged. That man!

She decided she needed to speak to someone else about the problem. Frances would do. She wasn't far away. No point calling Robert. He could be in London by now, for all she knew. Besides, he never answered the phone himself. You always had to go through some secretary or other to reach him. He spent his life in interminable meetings. No. It would have to be Frances.

★   ★   ★

The person Kate had in mind, Frances Murray, lived in a cottage just a hundred yards or so away from Kate's own. As usual, early as it was, she was pottering in her front garden when Kate arrived. Elderly though she might be, she was still pretty fit and she was a dedicated gardener, specialising in roses.

'Good morning, Frances!'

Frances straightened up and shaded her eyes with one hand. 'Good morning, my dear! How are you?'

'Annoyed, if you want the truth. Have you got a minute to spare me?'

Frances chuckled and said, 'Come on inside. I'm just about ready for a cup of coffee. You can join me.'

'Thank you.'

Kate paused to survey the border where Frances had been working. The earth freshly turned. Not a weed in sight.

'Would you like a job, Frances? I could do with some help. I have far too much work to do on my own.'

'No, thank you!' Frances said firmly. 'I am long and happily retired. Can't you find someone in the village to help?'

'Not yet.' Kate shook her head. 'I've tried, but so far I haven't found anyone suitable. The youngsters all want to work at a computer all day, or be fashion models or footballers. They have no interest in plants, still less in digging weed-infested ground and hauling paving slabs around.'

'What about some of the older men, the ones with allotments, perhaps?'

'They could do the work, but the trouble with them is they don't like working for a woman. They all want to tell me how to do the job. You've no idea how much that slows the work down.'

Frances laughed and steered her to a chair at the kitchen table. 'Well, it is unusual, I suppose. A young woman with her own landscaping business.'

'Garden design and renovation, please,' Kate said firmly. 'I would need a JCB and all sorts of other heavy machinery to do landscaping.'

'Whatever you call what you do, you're obviously doing very well indeed if you need more help. That can't be bad.'

'No. You're quite right. I'm very

pleased with how things have developed the past couple of years.'

'What about your young man? Couldn't he help you?'

'Robert? Oh, no!' Kate laughed and shook her head. 'Robert wouldn't want to get his hands dirty. Besides, he doesn't like wearing dirty old clothes. Smart-casual is the lowest he'll sink. He's a city man, is Robert.'

Frances chuckled. 'You shouldn't exaggerate so! He's a charming person. I'm sure he would help if you asked him nicely and told him you were desperate.'

'Possibly.'

Frances prepared the coffee and placed it on the table. 'Now,' she said, 'what are you so agitated about this beautiful morning — apart from the lack of help with your gardening, that is?'

'Well might you ask! I bumped into a very rude and aggressive young man in the grounds of Hillside House this morning. He claims to be the owner, and he shouted at me for trespassing, would you believe?

'I have no idea who he is. A trespasser himself, I assume. You haven't heard about anyone buying or moving in there, have you?'

Frances pursed her lips and shook her head. 'No, I haven't. Oh, dear! What an experience.'

'It certainly was,' Kate confirmed. 'I was shocked. So when I got home I rang the police. They said they would look into it. Goodness knows how long that will take, though. I was talking to a woman who might have been a hundred miles away, for all she seemed to know about this village. She probably was, in fact. Oh, why can't we just have a village bobby!'

'Those days are long gone, I'm afraid,' Frances said with a sympathetic sigh.

'Wouldn't it be better, though?'

'Yes, I think it would. But it's not going to happen. This man you met. Were you able to describe him to the police?'

'Not very well. He did give his name, but I can't remember what he said. It was foreign, though, a foreign sounding name. Not that that means much these days, I suppose. But he spoke perfectly good English — enough to shout at me, anyway.'

'Well, I'm sure he meant no harm. Just one of those things, I suppose.'

'Not to me, it wasn't,' Kate said, surprised by Frances's casual response. 'I've never known anything like it.'

'No, of course you haven't,' Frances said hurriedly. 'It must have been upsetting for you.'

'Very. If I'd had a spade with me I would probably have hit him with it.'

'Oh no! Surely not? Look, I'm really sorry about all this,' Frances said, as if now she was taking personal responsibility for the incident. 'It must have been most unpleasant for you.'

'It was. Not that it was your fault, Frances,' she added with a grin. 'I tell you what, though. I might have been shocked, but that man's going to have a bigger shock when the police arrive to arrest him!'

'You don't suppose he really is the new owner?'

'I don't. Not at all. Goodness knows who and what he is.'

3

Despite Frances's apparent lack of overwhelming concern, Kate couldn't get the man at Hillside House out of her mind. She certainly didn't think it was just one of those things. To her, it was diabolical! What a thing to have happened.

What did he say his name was? She frowned as she concentrated. Costas? Something Costas? It sounded Greek. She shook her head. She wasn't sure. Not that it mattered much. But she still felt a need to do something about him, whoever he was, and whatever his name was.

On her way to her current client's house, to do a little more work on their garden, she called in at the estate agent's office in the village. Jack Reynolds was always good to talk to if you wanted to know what was happening in the area.

As he rightly said, he kept his finger on the button. Not much escaped his attention.

'Morning, Jack.'

'Kate!' He said with his customary sunny smile. 'To what do I owe this unexpected, yet very welcome, visit? No, don't tell me! You want me to sell your charming little cottage for you?'

'That'll be the day! No. Sorry. I'm staying exactly where I am. I love my cottage. You'll have to put up with me forever.'

'Pity.' He looked solemn for a moment. Then the smile beamed out again. 'But at least that means you're not contemplating leaving us. That's a relief. You had me worried for a moment.'

'Jack Reynolds!' she said with resignation. 'Your mother must have had you kiss the Blarney Stone as soon as you were born.'

'Twice,' he shot back. 'Just to make sure it had taken.'

She smiled patiently and shook her

head. He was a rascal. Always teasing. Gift of the gab, and a salesman's patter to go with it.

'Jack, try to be serious for a moment, please. There's something I wanted to ask you. Have you heard anything about Hillside House, that old place next door to me, being sold recently?'

'Not a thing. It's not even been on the market, as far as I know. Why? Thinking of buying it?'

She shook her head. 'It's just that this morning, as I was wandered through the grounds — as I often do, with it being open to all and sundry — I was intercepted by a man who claimed I was trespassing on his property. I've never seen him before, and he was very rude and aggressive, quite frighteningly so. He even threatened to set the police on me.'

'Oh, Colonel Fenwick's come back to life, has he? I always said he would.'

Kate smiled reluctantly, and willed herself to ignore the facetious comments. They were just something you had to put up with in conversation with Jack Reynolds.

'Sorry, Kate. You have no idea who this fellow was?'

'None at all.' She shook her head and added, 'He said — I think — that his name was something Costas, a Greek-sounding name, not that I'm a linguist or anything.

'I'm thinking he was either a burglar or a squatter. Frances Murray doesn't seem to be bothered much, but I certainly am. The police can't be bothered either. I notified them as soon as I got in the house, but so far as I know they haven't been to investigate yet.'

Jack Reynolds frowned with thought and shook his head. 'Whoever he was, I've not heard anything. And I'm sure I would have if Hillside House had changed hands, or even been put on the market. You can't keep things like that quiet in a place like this.'

'That's what I was thinking. Who owns it now, actually? I've often wondered.'

'No idea. Since the old colonel passed away, it's just slipped off the radar.'

'Is it possible to find out?'

'Yes, of course. You can find that out by checking with the Land Registry. They keep a record of ownership for every property in the country. It would cost you twenty quid to inquire, mind.

'The trouble is that if Hillside House has been sold recently, the change of ownership might not have been recorded yet. They're supposed to keep everything up to date, but there's bound to be a delay at times. Do you want me to have a look for you?'

She hesitated. 'No, don't bother just now, Jack. Thanks all the same. I'll wait to hear what the police have to say before I spend any money on it.'

'Well, just let me know if you change your mind. And if that fellow turns up again and gives you any trouble, just give me a ring. I can be up there in no time.'

'Thanks, Jack. I appreciate the offer.'

George Matthews, her client, wasn't home, but she hadn't really expected him to be. She had just hoped that he might be. He was someone else she could usefully have talked to about Hillside House.

'He said he would probably pop in at lunch-time,' George's wife said, 'if that's any help?'

Kate pursed her lips and thought for a moment. Then she shook her head. 'It doesn't matter, Mrs Matthews. If I'm here when he comes, I'll have a word with him. If not, I'll phone tonight. It's not about the job anyway. I know what you both want doing. I'll just get on with it.'

'Please do. Summer's coming soon, and I can't wait to see the new garden.'

Kate smiled and turned away to get to work.

What the Matthews family wanted from her was very simple. They wanted their long-neglected, muddy waste tip converted into a place of beauty and delight, and they wanted it child-proof — and soon! Kate wasn't entirely sure she could come up with a design that would accommodate tender plants and mountain bikes, a perfect lawn and football, but she was certainly prepared to give it her best shot. She needed the money.

Needless to say, she was doing the actual work on the ground as well as the design. As she started manoeuvring patio slabs, she was reminded yet again of her dire need for assistance — but not from the likes of Frances. She needed someone more robust than that to help her. Someone more accustomed to hard physical labour than Robert, too. Surely there was someone out there who needed a job?

For a time the work absorbed her. The paving area she was laying down was next to the house, which was where she believed small children would want to be most of the time. So the plan was to make this a resilient area that was attractive to them. Then the delicate plants, further down the garden, might last a little longer. She had her doubts about that, having met the Matthews kids, but her client was made of more optimistic stuff.

★　★　★

'That will do it beautifully! An absolutely splendid job you're doing, Kate.'

She straightened up and spun round. Graham Matthews had arrived.

'Hello, Graham,' she said, smiling. 'You're back early. I wasn't expecting to see you today.'

'No office could detain me on a glorious day like this.'

'So you bunked off?'

'Exactly. If my kids can do it, why can't I occasionally?'

He was not an exact replica of Jack Reynolds, being quite portly and losing his hair, but his style of conversation suggested they could have been cousins. For the second time that morning she had to pretend it was a style that didn't exasperate her. These men! They were worse than Robert, and that was saying something.

'Graham, there was something I wanted to ask you. So I'm glad you've arrived. This morning I was intercepted by a strange man in the grounds of Hillside House, next door to me. I have no idea who he is, but he accused me of trespassing on his property. Very unpleasantly, I might add. In fact, we had an angry little row about it.

'Now, as you probably know, Hillside House has been empty for many years. But could someone possibly have acquired it without the fact being generally known? To put it another way, is it possible to check this man's claim to be the owner?'

Graham Matthews was a solicitor. He had a small practice in a neighbouring town, and from all accounts was rather good at his profession. So she had high hopes that he could find answers to her questions.

Now he cheerfully considered what she'd had to say before suggesting, 'Contact the Land Registry. They'll know. You can do it online. Just Google them, and follow the instructions. It's not difficult, but you do have to pay a fee, I seem to remember.'

She nodded. 'Jack Reynolds also suggested that. But he said they might not be up to date if there had been a recent sale, and I didn't want to waste my money by launching a premature inquiry with them. Is there no other way?'

'Short of knowing who the respective parties are, and who their solicitors are, I can't think of any. The County Council will be chasing any new occupant of Hillside House for their council tax eventually, but I can't imagine them being ahead of the Land Registry people.

'Anyway,' he concluded, 'the chap you saw this morning will probably be gone by now. He'll just have been a scrap metal merchant nosing around for easy pickings, I wouldn't be surprised. He didn't have a horse and cart, did he?'

'Not that I noticed.'

She smiled and shook her head. But the suggestion seemed a sensible one. She hadn't thought of it herself. A scrap metal merchant was a very plausible possibility. Scrap men, legal or not, seemed to have been creating havoc all over the country in recent years, stripping lead off church roofs, stealing cables and pipework, and one thing or another.

Graham added, 'They even took a big Henry Moore bronze from somewhere down south the other year. A priceless work of art, and it's believed to have been melted down for its scrap value. Just imagine! Hillside House would seem like a wonderful opportunity to people capable of doing things like that.'

Smiling ruefully, Kate agreed.

'Why didn't I think of that?' she said with a sigh. 'I just hope the police are on the scene before any damage is done.'

As she made her way home, the conversation stayed in her mind. Hillside House probably would seem like a treasure chest to a scrap man. She had never been inside, but she could imagine a house that age containing all sorts of things worth collecting by someone in the scrap metal trade. Radiators, a metal bath, kitchen equipment . . . The list of possibilities was endless.

Then there was the stuff scattered around the grounds: wrought-iron gates, fence posts, a vehicle in the garage, perhaps? She shook her head and gritted her teeth. The sooner this business was sorted out, the better — and the happier she would be.

4

That afternoon, when she returned home, Kate found a message from the police on her phone. Would she call them back?

She did so, to be told that an officer had visited Hillside House and spoken to the owner, a Mr Costas, who had said that there was no problem, and no reason at all for any of his neighbours to be concerned. End of story. Thank you for calling Northumbria Police!

Kate grimaced and muttered a few choice words under her breath. Then she took stock, and decided she was still not satisfied. What right had this Mr Costas to declare himself the owner of Hillside House? Who had given him that right? Was it even true?

Without giving it any more thought, she followed the advice that both Jack Reynolds and Graham Matthews had given her. She switched on her computer and looked for the website of the Land Registry.

Overcoming her annoyance at having to pay a fee, she paid for a search that revealed that a Mr Costas was indeed the owner of Hillside House, and had been for over two years.

Two years? That made her pause for thought. How could it be possible? How had he obtained ownership anyway? Neither she nor anyone she had spoken to had heard of it ever being on the market.

And if this Costas man had owned the property for that length of time, why had he only now appeared on the scene? It didn't make sense.

Something else that didn't make much sense was that the previous owner had been a Mrs Fenwick. She had apparently come into possession of the property a few years earlier, presumably after the colonel's death. But who on earth was she?

In normal circumstances, she would

simply have been the colonel's widow, of course. Yet Kate had always understood, having been told as much by more than one person in Callerton, that Colonel Fenwick had been a bachelor, and one without any siblings. So where had a Mrs Fenwick come from?

Perhaps she was a distant member of the family, one who happened to have the Fenwick name? That wasn't impossible. For instance, the colonel had not had a brother, by all accounts, but his own father might have done, and such a brother would have borne the family name. So would any male descendant of his, and any wives, of course. Could that be how a Mrs Fenwick had come into being? It was certainly possible.

Oh, what to think? She just didn't know.

Feeling somewhat overwhelmed by so much surprise information and speculation, and quite unable to see where to go from here, she put it all aside for the moment. To clear her head, she undertook some savage pruning in her rose garden, gritting her teeth as thorns tore at her arms. It was nearly as good distraction therapy as digging in heavy clay.

After tea she decided to visit Frances again. The questions just wouldn't go away, and Frances seemed the person most likely to be able to answer them. At least, Kate couldn't think of anyone better to ask.

'Am I interrupting anything?' she asked when Frances came to the door.

'Like what? A party, perhaps?' Frances laughed and opened the door wide. 'Come on in, dear. No, you're not interrupting anything at all. Besides, I'm always happy to see you.'

Frances's little cottage always seemed so cosy, and so it did that evening. Kate looked round the living room with an envious eye, admiring the furniture that fitted the space beautifully, the three original water colours on the wall of local landscapes and Frances's collection of fine porcelain carefully arranged in its cabinet.

'It always looks so nice in here,' she said wistfully, 'and so well arranged. Just perfect, in fact! I do try with my place, but I never seem to be able to get things quite right somehow.'

'Oh, you don't have the time that I have,' Frances said with a smile. 'I have nothing better to do.'

'No, it's not that,' Kate said, shaking her head. 'I think the difference is that you're a real countrywoman. I'm just pretending to be one.'

'Fiddlesticks! You do amazingly well in the time you have available. Anyway, I wasn't always a countrywoman, you know. I'm a bit of a fraud, really.'

Kate laughed and pointed to the knitting that had been laid aside on a small work table. 'A sweater?'

'Indeed. Knitting keeps my fingers nimble. Besides, there's nothing on the television I want to watch these days. It's all football or horrible news programmes about people doing nasty things to one another, not always in far-away countries either. Cup of tea, dear?'

'That would be lovely. Thank you. Want me to help?'

'Not at all. Just sit yourself down. You'll have had a hard day again, I expect?'

'Not really. But I'll tell you all about it when you come back.'

The sweater was well on the way. Obviously it was for winter. Chunky wool, and double-knit. From across the room, it looked a bit on the large size for Frances. A lot on the large size, in fact. Perhaps she was planning on wearing it over other things, the way you did in winter when the cold winds started to blow and frost formed on the windows.

She wondered if Frances was one of those old dears who were reluctant to turn the heating up when it got cold. She wouldn't have been surprised. Perhaps she ought to watch out for her when winter came round again. She didn't want her perishing from hypothermia just because she was too stubborn to reach for the thermostat.

Some old people couldn't afford to turn the heating up, she knew, but there were plenty who could and still didn't. It was as if it was a matter of honour and pride not to acknowledge hardship in any way. Either that or they distrusted central heating still. The older generation, eh! she thought with a grin. What were they like?

'What are you smiling about?' Frances asked suspiciously when she returned with a tea tray. 'Has something happened while I've been in the kitchen?'

Kate laughed. 'Frances! What a suspicious mind you have. Nothing at all has happened. I was just wondering if you were knitting such a warm jumper because you don't like turning the heating up in winter. Is that it?'

'Not at all,' Frances said sharply. 'But I do admit that I'm not overly fond of a house that's too hot.'

'Hm. I know what that means. I'm going to watch you next winter, and make sure you turn the heating on. I'm warning you!'

Frances laughed and shook her head. 'Anyway, what have you been up to today? Anything much?'

'It's been a very interesting day, actually. This business about Hillside House has been on my mind ever since that man appeared the other morning.'

'Oh, you don't want to worry about him! I'm sure he didn't mean any harm.'

'That's all very well, Frances, but how would you know that? Who is he anyway? And what about his claim that Hillside House is his property?'

'I don't know, I'm sure,' Frances said with a sigh as she began to pour the tea. 'I suppose you're right.'

'Anyway,' Kate said, pressing on, 'I spoke to Jack Reynolds, who says he hasn't heard anything about Hillside House being sold, or even put on the market. Then I spoke to Graham Matthews, the solicitor. Nothing there either. Meanwhile, the police got back to me to say they had spoken to this Mr

Costas — the owner, they called him! — and everything was in order.'

'Well, there you are, then. There's nothing to worry about.'

'Frances, you're so trusting! I still wasn't convinced. So I got on to the Land Registry people, as both Jack and Graham had suggested, and found that this Mr Costas really is the legal owner. He has been for two years. Can you imagine?'

Frances smiled and shook her head. 'Not really. Is the tea to your taste, dear?'

'Perfectly, thank you,' Kate said, nodding, even though she hadn't even tasted it yet. 'Then I found something else out. Before this Mr Costas appeared on the scene, a Mrs Fenwick was the owner. How about that! I thought the old colonel was a bachelor. Didn't you tell me that yourself?'

Frances looked uncomfortable. 'Oh, you can't take everything I say at face value, dear. The old memory's not what it was, I'm afraid. Half the time, I don't know what I'm talking about these days.'

'Nonsense! I'm not having that. You're bright as a button, Frances. So even you never heard of Colonel Fenwick having a wife?'

Reluctantly, it seemed, Frances shook her head.

'I wonder if he was married all along?' Kate mused. 'Or perhaps he went on a secret holiday to Thailand, and got himself one of those Thai brides I keep reading about?'

'Colonel Fenwick?' Frances laughed. 'Oh, no! Not him. He wasn't like that at all.'

'Oh? So what was he like?'

Frances shrugged. 'A crusty old bachelor, who liked things just the way they were, and always had been. He had a good life, I believe, and he didn't want anything to change.'

'Not even his garden, from the looks of it,' Kate said with a sniff. 'Not much work has been done there for half a century, I shouldn't think.'

'I'm sure he did his best, dear.' Frances smiled gently and added, 'He was a good man.'

'I'm sure he was,' Kate said with a shrug. 'But where did Mrs Fenwick come from? And what about this Mr Costas? That's what I'd like to know. It's quite a mystery, you have to admit.'

Frances smiled indulgently. 'More tea, dear?' she asked sweetly.

Kate felt as if she was being patted on the head to soothe her.

5

Jack Reynolds was surprised to hear about the new owner of Hillside House.

'In fact,' he admitted, 'I'm darned annoyed. No-one told me it had changed hands, or even that it had been on the market. How could that have happened? I'm the only estate agent for miles around.'

Kate pursed her lips and frowned thoughtfully. 'It's not on, is it?'

'I must be losing my touch. Costas, you say? He's the owner now?'

She nodded and waited, sensing that Jack was becoming ever more intrigued, as well as annoyed, which was exactly what she wanted him to be.

'Before this Mr Costas got the place,' she added provocatively, 'it was owned by a Mrs Fenwick.'

'Who? Oh, no! I'm not having that,' Jack said, shaking his head in vigorous denial. 'There wasn't any Mrs Fenwick!'

He's really outraged now, Kate thought with satisfaction. He'll want to know what's been going on just as much as I do.

'It's all in the Land Registry file,' she added. 'I took your advice and looked it up. But wasn't the colonel a bachelor?'

'Indeed he was.'

'And Frances Murray told me he had no brothers or sisters. So who could this Mrs Fenwick have been? She must have been related in some way, don't you think, but how? I can't think of an explanation.'

'Right,' Jack said grimly. 'I'd better get to the bottom of this. I need to know what's been going on around here. Leave it with me, Kate.'

Gladly! she thought happily as she left the premises. Jack Reynolds was far better equipped and connected than she was to find answers to these troubling questions.

Besides, she had a lot of work to do

today, whereas all he had to do was sit in his office and wait for someone wanting to buy or sell a house to come through the door. Such an event did not, she suspected, happen all that often. Once a year, probably.

★ ★ ★

Back at home that afternoon, Kate saw her new neighbour again. He seemed to be inspecting the remains of the fence that at one time had firmly separated his property from hers. Either that or he was just being nosy and wanting to see what she was up to. She wasn't having that.

She parked her pick-up and walked over to him. 'Can I help you?'

'No,' he said, shaking his head.

She stared at him over the thin screen of low-growing shrubbery that separated them. Part of her wished there was still an eight-foot timber fence between them. It wouldn't be much to look at, but it would be easier to defend and she would probably feel safer.

He shrugged and said, 'This fence is no good. It must be fixed.'

'And so it will be one day, when I get round to it. I'm a bit busy at the moment. You're still here, then?'

'Still here? Of course I am here. Why shouldn't I be?'

'No reason at all, if you really are the new owner.'

He scowled at her. 'You told the police to investigate me?'

'I did. As far as I was concerned, you were a trespasser — possibly a dangerous one. At the very least, you had been very threatening towards me. I wasn't going to let you get away with that.'

'You were in my house. I found you!'

'No, you didn't. Not in your house. I've never been inside Hillside House in my entire life. I was walking through the grounds. That was all.'

'Same thing.'

'It's not at all the same thing. The grounds have more or less been open to public access for years. Probably since the last owner died. It's just like a park. Everybody walks through.

'Anyway, you can see for yourself that the fences and walls wouldn't keep anybody out, and there are no gates anymore.'

She realised then that he was growing increasingly exasperated, and decided she had better tone it down a bit. She didn't want to have to fight him physically, at least not yet. She would leave that to a time when all other options had been exhausted.

'I will stop you good,' he declared, glowering at her. 'I will fix this fence myself — and put up gates. I will keep you out. Everybody will be kept out!'

'One day?'

'Yes. One day I will do it.' He paused, thought about it and added, 'And I will put barbed wire on top. Barbed wire is very effective — and very nice, I think.'

Overcoming her horror at the idea, she suddenly wondered if this man was laughing at her. Surely he couldn't be serious?

'Barbed wire?'

'Much, much barbed wire. Rolls of it. Maybe razor wire, too.'

'And guard dogs?' she asked.

'Guard dogs, yes. Guard dogs are a good idea; maybe a cannon, too.'

'Don't forget the land mines!' she said sharply, turning to walk away.

What an extraordinary person, she thought, shaking her head. He's demented! What a wonderful next-door neighbour I've acquired.

★ ★ ★

'What does he look like?' Frances asked, when Kate went to tell her the latest news.

'How do you mean?'

'Well, is he young, old? Is he handsome? Fat, thin?'

'Oh, Frances, really! I couldn't care less what he looks like. He could be obese and bald, for all I care. In fact, if he was pleasant with it, that would be preferable.'

'Just wondering,' Frances said with a shrug. 'More tea?'

'No, thank you. I'd better get home. I'm swimming in tea.'

'You can never have too much tea, I always think.' Frances poured herself another cup and added, 'Perhaps you'll get used to your new neighbour? I shouldn't worry so much, dear.'

'You don't live next to him!'

Kate got to her feet. 'Sorry, Frances. That was uncalled for. Perhaps I will get used to him. I'll have to, won't I?'

'That's the spirit! Live and let live.'

'I'm not having the barbed wire, though.'

'No, of course not. I'm sure he didn't mean it anyway.'

Kate nodded. 'Perhaps not. I suppose I did aggravate him a bit. If it helps, he's not too bad-looking, I suppose. Perhaps more your type than mine, though,' she added with a grin.

Frances laughed and shooed her out of the door.

Whyever had she said that? Kate

thought, smiling to herself as she made her way home. It was the truth, though. Mr Costas was quite handsome, she supposed, with his black hair, tanned face and athletic build. Probably in his late thirties. And he had those extraordinarily piercing blue eyes that might be attractive if he were not so angry. Ideal toy boy for Frances!

The thought made her laugh out loud. So she was in a good mood by the time she reached home and found that Jack Reynolds had left a message on her phone.

6

'I haven't got to the bottom of it yet,' Jack Reynolds said when Kate rang him back, 'but it's right enough. This Mr Costas does own Hillside House now. Goodness knows how that's come about, though.

'As for who this Mrs Fenwick is, or was, your guess is as good as mine. I'm no further forward. Have you seen anything more of Costas, by the way?'

'I saw him just this afternoon, actually. We exchanged a few more words.'

Jack chuckled. 'Choice ones, I hope?'

'Not friendly, anyway. Let's leave it at that. I don't know what to make of him. I'm coming to the conclusion that the man is mad.'

'That's all we need around here! As if we didn't have enough mad men.'

'Who else have you got in mind?'

'That man up at Woodside Farm, Willy Armstrong.'

'Why? What's he been up to?'

'He won't pay his bill; says he'll cover my car with cow muck if I keep on bothering him about it.'

'What you need is Mr Costas to protect your car. He's just threatened to put razor wire and guard dogs around his property to keep me and everybody else out.'

'Has he now? What did you say to that?'

'I told him to put in land mines, as well. They would help.'

Jack paused for a moment and then began laughing. 'Is he serious?'

'You tell me! I think so, though.'

'I'll have to have a word with him. I'll see if he'll go and see Willy Armstrong about that bill.'

'Good luck with that, Jack.'

So she wasn't any further forward, but at least Jack had confirmed what she had found out for herself. Hillside House did indeed have a new owner.

Unfortunately, she now had to accept that it really was Mr Costas. That was more than just a nuisance, but she was going to have get used to the fact.

'What about the mysterious Mrs Fenwick? Do we really know nothing at all about her?

'I'm afraid not. I have an address for her, though. She lives in Cheltenham, apparently. Or she used to, at least.'

'As she would, wouldn't she?'

'What? Oh, yes. If she was a colonel's widow, you mean? Yes. There'll be a lot of them there, I shouldn't wonder. Cheltenham's the sort of place where they are likely to congregate. Anyway, here it is.'

He read out an address and then added, 'Sorry, Kate. I have to get on now. There's a new client I need to see this evening, and he lives some distance away.'

'Goodness, Jack! Another new client? You had one of them just last year, didn't you?'

'Very funny. That's what I like about

you, Kate — your sense of humour. I'll miss that when I've sold that cottage for you.'

'Ha, ha! One tries. One does one's best. Thanks, Jack!'

She ended the call, giggling, as Jack launched into his set-piece about how his practice was the best in the valley. The only one in the valley, and for miles beyond, she managed not to say.

* * *

Preparing supper took her a little while. For once, she had decided she would have a proper meal. Her hard work that day had earned it. Pasta it would be, with a sauce she liked and sometimes managed to buy from the deli in town. A rare treat. One, she had to acknowledge, that Robert wouldn't have been thrilled about. Robert liked real meat, as he called it. But Robert wasn't here, was he?

No doubt he would be wining and

dining one of his posh clients somewhere. Perhaps he would call her
tonight. If not, she would call him.
Sometimes his work kept him away
longer than she liked, but there it was.
They both had careers to manage.

* * *

As she ate, her eyes kept returning to
the scrap of paper on which she had
written the address Jack Reynolds had
given her. Cheltenham. It was a long
way away. She had been there once, and
she recalled that it was one of those spa
towns, like Harrogate and Royal Leam-
ington Spa. Like Perth, too, north of
the border. Exactly the sort of place
where the widow of a retired army
officer might settle, if indeed that was
what Mrs Fenwick was.

But was that what she was? Could
the colonel have been married, after all?
Or was this unknown woman a distant
relative with the family name who had
inherited the property? She could, after

all, be the wife or widow of a cousin of the colonel's. No reason at all why she couldn't be. And that seemed the most likely explanation, when you thought about it.

Oh, come on! she admonished herself. You just don't know. That's the truth of it. And there's no point speculating. You have to find out who and what Mrs Fenwick is, or was. And there's only one way to do that. You have to get up off your bottom and do something!

At least Jack Reynolds had given her somewhere to start. She had an address for the lady. A short burst of activity on the internet took her a little further. For a Mrs Fenwick at the address in Cheltenham she found a phone number. Magic!

She took a few moments out then to make a cup of coffee and think about what she was going to say. Then she took the plunge and dialled the number.

A woman answered. She sounded

young and harassed. In the background, children were making a lot of noise.

'Oh, hello!' Kate said brightly. 'Is that Mrs Fenwick?'

'Who?'

'Mrs Fenwick.'

'No, it isn't. You've got the wrong number, I'm afraid.'

'This is the number I have for her,' Kate said hastily, hoping to prevent the woman ending the call.

'Look, our name is Jenkinson. I have no idea who the woman you want is.'

'My name is Kate Jackson.' She took a deep breath to calm herself before she went on. 'I'm anxious to reach Mrs Fenwick, and I understood that she was the owner of this property. She must have moved. Can I ask how long you've been living there?'

'A year. Look, this is a busy time for me. I haven't got time . . . '

'I'm very sorry, Mrs Jenkinson. But this really is important. Can I ask if you bought the house off Mrs Fenwick, and if you know where she moved to?'

'House? It's not a house. I don't know where you got that idea. It's a block of flats! And we're just renting, like everyone else in the building. There's twenty-six flats.'

Ah! Kate winced. She really had got off to a bad start. No wonder the poor woman was irritated.

'Can I ask who you rent from?'

The woman sighed wearily. 'Mr Prescott. He's an estate agent in town. I'm sorry. I've got to go!'

'You wouldn't have a phone number or an address for him, I suppose?'

'I've got to go!'

She broke off to scream instructions to a child who seemed to be having toilet problems. Kate winced, visualising the catastrophe that seemed to be unfolding in a flat in elegant Cheltenham.

'Saville Place,' the woman said wearily, coming back to the phone. 'That's where his office is. Right in the centre. Sorry. I really do have to go now. I've got one on the toilet, and my baby needs feeding as well.'

'Thank you, Mrs Jenkinson. You've been really helpful. I'm very sorry to have kept you so long.'

Her apology was wasted. The call had been ended. Kate shrugged and switched her phone off. She felt very sorry for Mrs Jenkinson, and a little guilty for keeping her talking so long. But what could she do? She gave a little sigh and put it behind her.

At least she was a little further along now. She had made some progress. It sounded as if Mrs Fenwick — whoever she was — owned an investment property in Cheltenham. How sensible. Just the kind of thing that a financially stable, old-style colonel's widow might do to guarantee a sufficient income in old age.

A glance at the clock told her it was too late to be calling the estate agent now, even if she could find his phone number. It would have to wait till morning, but she would call him then.

She was beginning to feel she was making progress, and it was a feeling that was very satisfying. This business with Mr Costas was a long way from being over, and she felt that Mrs Fenwick might well be the key to unlocking the puzzle.

Then the phone rang, startling her. She stared at it, wondering if it was Mrs Jenkinson in Cheltenham ringing back, perhaps to threaten to sue her for wasting her time — or seeking recompense for a blocked toilet!

7

'It's me. I'm in Leeds, Kate. It's got later than I'd intended. So don't expect to see me tonight.'

'OK, Robert. Thanks for letting me know. How's it going?'

She had only the flimsiest idea of what he was doing there. Something to do with a shopping centre. A big project anyway.

'I don't think it's going to happen,' Robert said, sounding disconsolate. 'They want too much for the site. I'll stay with it, in case I can get them to come down, but I don't think the figures are ever going to work on this one.'

'So you'll pull out?'

'Well . . . yes, basically. We'll have to. There's no point taking on a project that will lose us money.'

No indeed, she thought. That wouldn't do at all. They could invest millions, and still lose money. It was very different to her own little business, and obviously a lot more difficult. Poor Robert.

'I've got one little bit of progress to report, though,' Robert added. 'I've made Mr Costas an offer for Hillside House, and he's considering it. I think he'll accept. That will improve my figures for the month.'

She gasped aloud. 'You've what?'

'Made him a firm offer. I got in touch with him today. He was definitely interested. You can always tell.'

'Interested in what, though?'

'If the deal comes off, I'll be looking to pull the old house down and build on the site, like I said. If I can't do that, I'll just build in the grounds anyway. I could get a lot of houses on that site.'

She was stunned, scarcely able to organise her thoughts, let alone speak. After all she had said when he first raised it? He was going ahead anyway?

'Robert, I don't want that to happen — any of it!'

He chuckled. 'I know. You told me. But that's progress, isn't it? Anyway, I have to go now. It looks as if the meeting is re-convening. See you tomorrow. Love you. Bye!'

The call had ended, she realised a moment later. Robert had gone. She hadn't even had time to say goodbye.

★ ★ ★

For a little while she thought over what Robert had said, trying to make sense of it. Why was he doing this? He knew she didn't want him making Hillside House one of his projects. They had talked about that — disagreed about it! — and she had told him how she felt. And yet he was going ahead anyway? He must have known — he did know! — she would be disappointed. So why do it?

What he had told her just made her feel utterly depressed. Perhaps he didn't really care for her, and her feelings, after all. Perhaps the only thing that mattered to him was his career, and making money.

Then, for no good reason, her mood suddenly lifted again. Of course! How silly she was. Robert had just been teasing her, hadn't he? That was all. He hadn't been in touch with Mr Costas at all. How could he have? There hadn't been enough time, and he didn't have his phone number anyway — assuming Mr Costas even had a phone.

Besides, there was no way Robert would just ignore her and go ahead with something when she had objected to it so strongly and repeatedly. After all, they loved each other, didn't they? People who loved each other didn't deliberately set out to hurt one another.

She smiled fondly. What was he like? Such a tease! She would have to find a way of getting her own back, preferably before he arrived tomorrow night.

* * *

The next morning, before she left home, she found the phone number of

68

the estate agent in Cheltenham and made a call.

'Mr Prescott?'

'One moment, please. I'll put you through. Who should I say is calling?'

'My name is Kate Jackson. But Mr Prescott doesn't know me.'

It didn't seem to matter. The call was diverted and picked up again with admirable speed, an indication perhaps that businesses were on their toes in these straitened times.

'Bob Prescott here, Miss Jackson. How can I help you?'

'Oh, good morning, Mr Prescott. I'm anxious to contact one of your clients, a Mrs Fenwick, who owns an apartment block in Cheltenham. I wondered if you would kindly give me contact details for her?'

After a brief but telling pause, she had her answer.

'I'm afraid we never give out information about any of our clients, Miss Jackson. May I ask who you represent, and what your interest is?'

'I don't represent anyone, Mr Prescott. Just myself. I live in Northumberland, in a village where Mrs Fenwick once owned a property next to my own. I wish to speak to her on matters of mutual interest.'

'Ah! So it's a retrospective planning matter?'

'No, not at all. Not at this stage, at least.'

'But it might be?'

'Well, I suppose it might, eventually. My immediate concern, though, is to do with the ownership of the property. I would like to speak to Mrs Fenwick about that. Perhaps I should add that it's not a financial issue. It's information I'm seeking, because what happens next door affects my property too.'

After another pause, presumably while he did some checking, Mr Prescott said that Mrs Fenwick was indeed one of his clients. Unfortunately, he could say nothing more. As he had already told her, he could not release information about a client, and certainly not over the telephone.

Kate grew frustrated. 'I only want to speak to her, Mr Prescott!'

'Even so. I'm sorry.'

His manner was growing colder by the moment. Clearly, not only was she not potential new business, she was proving to be a nuisance, possibly a considerable nuisance. Perhaps even a danger to the financial interests of his client.

Kate tried a new approach.

'In that case, could I ask you to pass on my contact details to Mrs Fenwick? Then she can make her own mind up about whether or not to speak to me.'

'You can certainly ask, Miss Jackson.'

She gave him the information.

'I will tell you, however,' he concluded, 'that it is most unlikely that my client will wish to speak to you. She has made it quite clear that she will not entertain approaches from anyone, either in person or by telephone.'

Exasperated, Kate almost snapped at him about such a stupid arrangement, but somehow she managed to curb her tongue. She couldn't afford to spoil whatever slim chance there was of making contact with Mrs Fenwick.

'Thank you, Mr Prescott. I'm most grateful,' she said sweetly.

'Not at all. Good day to you, Miss Jackson.'

Pompous ass! She hurled the phone away from her and sat glowering at the kitchen wall. What now?

* * *

For a while she busied herself with the garden design she was developing for a client. Using some new software she had acquired recently, she mapped bands of colour, trying out different arrangements at a very broad scale before she got down to the detailed business of choosing and naming the plant species and varieties she would recommend. It was a phase of work she always enjoyed, creating the broad-brush ideas before the hard work started.

This time, though, she wasn't enjoying what she was doing. She was too distracted. The names kept creeping into her mind from the murky edge where she had consigned them: Mrs Fenwick, Mr Costas, Mr Prescott. Oh, why couldn't they leave her alone for five minutes!

She switched off the computer and made herself a mug of coffee that she took outside. It was a lovely morning. Overnight drizzle had made everything in the garden gleam and sparkle, and now the heat was building as the sun rose in a clear blue sky. By late morning it would be really hot, too hot for labouring in somebody's overgrown garden.

She grimaced. What was wrong with her? This was no way to be. She had to get on, and do something. Fretting and worrying about Mr Costas and Mrs Fenwick all the hours that God sent was not going to put much in her bank account by the end of the month.

If only that pompous man in

Cheltenham had been a bit more forthcoming and sensible! She might have been able to clear all this mystery away if she'd had the chance to talk to Mrs Fenwick for five minutes.

Oh, well, she thought with a sigh. It wasn't going to happen, was it? She might as well go to see Florence. She needed someone to talk to, and unfortunately for Florence she was the nearest friend she had. After that, it might be possible to get some work done.

8

Frances could manage to do most things herself still, despite her advanced age, but one thing she couldn't do was mend her own car when it went wrong. Living where they did, cars that didn't work were a huge problem, if not normally a catastrophe. The village had no bus service any longer, not since the bus services had been privatized, and walking or cycling were not always good options for the elderly or for people with a handicap of some sort.

Kate wasn't in the least bit surprised to find Frances in a fury over her ancient Volvo's refusal to start. But she kept a straight face. She sensed it wasn't a laughing matter.

'The stupid thing!' her normally gentle old neighbour snapped, looking as if she wanted to give the car a good kicking.

'Frances! Whatever's the matter?'

'It won't go.'

Kate winced and steeled herself. She recognised the need to be diplomatic. It wasn't often Frances lost her temper, but when she did she could still create a considerable storm.

'Flat battery, perhaps?'

'No. There's nothing wrong with the battery.'

'Damp spark plugs?'

'In the heat we've been having? Diesel engines don't have spark plugs anyway.' That last remark was made in a dismissive tone that amounted to a rebuke. Kate winced and tried to focus on being helpful. But she had almost reached the end of her technical knowledge. How could she be expected to know that about diesel engines? It was news to her. If it came to that, how did a little old lady like Frances know?

She struggled to suggest anything else. Then she realised Frances would probably not welcome any more suggestions anyway. She definitely would not be interested in a technical discussion about the internal combustion engine with someone who knew nothing at all about the subject. Frances didn't suffer fools gladly at the best of times, and especially when she was not feeling full of sweetness and light.

'Have you phoned the garage?' Kate asked, failing to think of anything else that might be helpful.

'Of course I have. They're supposed to be coming — when they have time!'

Oh, dear. Kate realised she was going to have to be even more tactful, if she was to avoid the full fury of Frances's scorn.

'Well, is there anywhere you need to be urgently this morning, Frances? I can take you.'

'No, you can't. You have work to do.'

'Frances, if there is somewhere you need to go, please tell me. Stop being so cantankerous. Let's go! The gardening can easily wait a while.'

'An ordinary person used to be able

to repair their own car,' Frances started up, ignoring Kate's suggestion. 'Yes, even a woman! At least, this one could. But who can mend a car now?

'You need a qualification in computing science as well as a degree in mechanical engineering before you can even open the bonnet!'

For a moment Kate amused herself with images of Frances in oily overalls crawling beneath a car, long spanner in one hand and a hammer in the other.

No, she decided reluctantly. It just didn't fit. Frances was a remarkable woman, but she couldn't see her doing that sort of thing.

'I could, you know,' Frances said, sensing Kate's doubts.

'Could what?'

'Mend my own car. When I was young, you had to be able to do that, especially if you were heading for remote places. In the desert there were no garages, never mind breakdown services. But with the old Morris Oxford you could fix it yourself, if you had to. And believe me, you often did have to! Even before you set off you had to clean the spark plugs. The sand got everywhere.'

Kate dimly recalled Frances once mentioning that in her youth she had spent a lot of time in the Middle East, the Gulf particularly. But right now didn't seem the time to go into that subject. Get a grip! she told herself.

'Frances, where do you need to be this morning? Anywhere in particular?'

'The doctor's, of course. I need mending, too. I'm no better than this stupid car!'

'Let's go, then. I'm ready when you are.'

★　★　★

The GP's surgery was several miles away, in the next village. On the drive there, to change the subject, Kate told Frances of her investigation into the situation at Hillside House.

'So this Mr Costas really does seem

to own the house,' she concluded.

'You didn't think he was just making it up, did you?' Frances said tartly.

'I did, actually. Like I said before, I thought he was a trespasser or a burglar. Or somebody up to no good anyway.'

'Oh, Kate! You worry too much. Let it go.'

'I worry too much? What about you, and that old car of yours? You should trade it in.'

'I've only had it ten years. There's nothing wrong with it.'

'This morning there is.'

'That's just one of those things. It's a bit temperamental, like me,' Frances added with a rueful smile. 'It doesn't often let me down.'

Only when it matters, Kate thought. An old car was an old car. But she knew she couldn't change Frances's mind.

'So what I did next,' she said, reverting to the topic of Hillside House, 'was look up this Mrs Fenwick who used to own Hillside House.'

There was a sigh and a pause then, as if Frances couldn't believe her ears.

'Oh, Kate! You didn't?'

'Oh, yes I did. And guess what I discovered?'

Frances said nothing for a moment. Then: 'What?'

'Nothing! Well, I discovered that she is alive still, and that she apparently lives in Cheltenham. Jack Reynolds found an address there for me.'

'The estate agent?'

'Yes. I thought who better to look for it. So next I found a phone number for that address, and phoned it. Unfortunately, it turns out that Mrs Fenwick doesn't actually live there. The address is a block of flats that she owns, and it's managed by an estate agent.

'I spoke to him, a Mr Prescott, but he wouldn't divulge any information about Mrs Fenwick. Nothing at all. He wouldn't even give me her contact details. I'm surprised he was even prepared to admit she existed.'

'Good for him!' Frances snapped.

'It's good to know some business people keep up proper ethical standards.'

'Yes, well. Perhaps. But it didn't help me. So I left my own details with him, and now I'm waiting to see if Mrs Fenwick contacts me.'

Frances was silent for a moment. Then she said, 'I do wish you would just leave it, Kate. You are wasting your valuable time pursuing questions that are nothing to do with you.'

'How can you say that, Frances? Mr Costas lives right next door to me! I want to know how he got ownership of Hillside House. It all seems very fishy to me.'

'But you have better things to do, surely?'

That was possibly true, Kate had to acknowledge. But the questions wouldn't go away, and she couldn't rest while they remained unanswered.

'Look, I'm determined to solve this mystery, Frances. I can't get on with anything while all this is hanging over me. Anyway, here we are. Don't worry about how long it takes. I'll wait for you.

'Oh, there was something else I wanted to tell you, by the way.'

'What's that?'

Kate grinned. 'Robert rang me up last night. He said he'd made Mr Costas an offer for Hillside House. He wants to pull it down and build a lot of new houses on the site.'

Frances stared for a moment and then said, 'Oh, dear. I rather like the old house.'

'So do I. Robert knows that, too.'

'Then why are you laughing?'

'Because I don't believe him, of course! He's just teasing.'

Frances shook her head and got out of the car. She slammed the door shut and hurried towards the entrance to the surgery. Kate had the feeling that Frances was frustrated and annoyed with her, Robert and quite possibly much of the rest of the world. It really was time she got herself a new car.

9

Kate began to see Mr Costas more and more often. Sometimes he would be strolling through the grounds of Hillside House. Often he would just be standing still, seeming to observe birds high in the trees, or even the trees themselves perhaps. She wondered, and at times even believed, he was watching, and studying, her. Probably he kept an eye on their other neighbours, too. It was as if he was struggling to adapt to living in Hillside House, which wasn't too surprising. For one man, a single person at that, which was what he appeared to be, and him a stranger, there would be a lot to take in about how people lived here.

When she was leaving home early one morning, she found him on the road outside her cottage. He stood, hands in his pockets, seemingly watching the world go by. She wondered if he was waiting for her to appear. Perhaps he wanted another round of verbal fisticuffs? If so, she was good and ready. But did he have no work to do, no job to go to?

She would have got straight into her pickup and driven away as usual, but she wanted to know what he was doing. She wanted, she supposed, to satisfy herself that he was not waiting for her to leave, so that he could break into her cottage or wreck her garden. She wouldn't put anything past him.

'Good morning!' she called, trying hard to avoid putting anything into her voice to suggest how much she hated and despised him.

'Yes, it is. Good morning.'

He turned and took a couple of paces towards her. Kate hesitated, and then took a few paces towards him. She wanted to stop him at the boundary between their respective properties. She did not want him entering her space. A public road it might be officially, but residents had always considered the space outside their own homes to be theirs. She was no different to anyone else in that respect.

'Are you settling in?' she asked with mock politeness, for all the world as if she were enquiring it of a normal new neighbour against whom she had not a single objection.

'Settling in?' He shook his head and chuckled. 'Is that what you think I am doing?'

'I have no idea what you are doing, Mr Costas,' she responded tartly, stung by his answer.

She began to turn away but he spoke again, delaying her.

'It is strange here,' he said. 'Unusual. Have you lived here for a long time?'

'A few years, yes. And there's nothing unusual about it. It's a perfectly normal lane in a perfectly normal Northumbrian village.'

He pursed his lips. She got the idea that he didn't agree but didn't know quite what to say next. He was trying to be civil, perhaps, but he just didn't know what to say to her. Well, that was all right. She didn't really want him speaking to her, and she certainly didn't want to speak to him. She had never met such a rude and arrogant man.

'Have you just bought Hillside House?' she asked nevertheless, deciding to help him out, in the interest of her own search for answers to questions that wouldn't go away.

'No.'

'Because I hadn't realised it was on the market — up for sale, I mean.'

'I know what you mean,' he said quickly, as if offended by her effort to translate such simple language.

'Truthfully,' he added with a sigh, relenting, 'I have owned this place for more than two years.'

'Oh?'

So he was prepared to tell her the truth about that, at least. Her interest was piqued.

'Yet you have only arrived here very recently?'

'Very recently, yes. From Cyprus. I have come from Cyprus to here, to Hillside House, in this unusual village.'

She ignored the repeated suggestion that Callerton was out of the ordinary. She was too astonished by the other part of his answer.

'Cyprus is your home?'

'It was. Yes. Cyprus. I have lived there all my life. I am Greek Cypriot.'

Another astonishing revelation. She thought quickly, eager to keep the information flowing.

'So what are you doing here?' she asked. 'I mean, what will you do with Hillside House, if you really do own it? Will you live here, Mr Costas?'

'I don't know.' He shrugged and smiled. 'I am Elek to my friends. Mr Costas only to police officers, and such people.'

Was that a dig at her for calling the police? Well, too bad! He'd had it coming.

'And I'm Kate,' she said, 'as I told you once before. Kate Jackson.'

'Ah, yes! When we first met. It was a bad day for me, that time. I was trying to get used to what I had found here, and I was tired, very tired. But now I find we are neighbours, yes?'

She nodded. It sounded like an apology, almost a gracious one. If so, it had been a long time coming. Still, it was welcome enough in its own way.

'Your boyfriend, Mr Elliot, is a very nice man, I think.'

'You have met Robert?'

He nodded. She was astonished. Suddenly, an unpleasant feeling stirred within her. What on earth was going on? What was Robert playing at?

'When?' she asked.

'Just the other day.' He shrugged and added, 'He made me an offer to buy Hillside House, a very good offer. He seems to want my house very badly. So I am considering his offer carefully.'

Suddenly she was furious, all her misgivings about Robert coming back to assault her. He hadn't been teasing her at all! He had meant it all along, and was quite happy to ignore her feelings about the matter.

'Don't you dare sell to him!' she demanded. 'If you sell Hillside House to Robert, I will never speak to you again — or to him either!'

Mr Costas looked astonished. He gazed at her with raised eyebrows, and a big question mark on his face.

'I mean it,' she warned.

'But surely it would be a good house for you to live in when you and Mr Elliot are married? It needs some work doing, of course, but that can be done.'

'Robert and I have no plan to marry. You are jumping to conclusions, Mr Costas. Besides, I have a house, a very wonderful house, already.'

He looked past her at the cottage. 'Only a small house,' he said, almost begging to differ.

'It's quite big enough for me,' she snapped. 'Now, if you'll excuse me, I must go to work.'

She was aware as she drove away that Mr Costas was looking very puzzled. Well, let him! Between him and Robert, she didn't know which of them was worse. Robert, probably.

The very thought of him going behind her back like this incensed her. Surely she had made her feelings clear enough? Surely he understood her point of view?

Well, if not, she was going to read the riot act to him. There was simply no way she wanted Hillside House to become part of Robert's portfolio of development projects. No way in the world!

10

When Robert came next, Kate was eager to talk to him about Hillside House. Why not? Her every waking moment seemed to revolve around it these days. Perhaps Frances was right when she said she was obsessing about the place, but she couldn't help it. Hillside House was important to her, and so was its future. She was determined to have a role in shaping what happened to it — or didn't happen to it!

'Have you heard from Mr Costas yet, Robert?'

'Not yet, no.' Robert shook his head. 'What's for supper?'

'Is lasagne all right? I had a long day today. There wasn't time to do anything complicated.'

'Lasagne is perfect.' Robert grinned. 'Anything would be after a day like I've just had! It's so good to be back here, and to see you again, Kate. Actually, it's been a long week for me, never mind a long day.'

'Were you able to salvage anything from the Leeds project?' she asked half-heartedly.

That wasn't what she really wanted to discuss, but she needed their conversation to stay calm and civilized. She wasn't going to blow what chance she had of influencing Robert by starting with a string of accusations.

Robert shook his head. 'It was a waste of time. The owners simply held out for far more money for their site than made sense, especially given the state of the economy at the moment. Good luck to them if they can get it, but the price was too steep for us. The project would have lost us money if we'd gone ahead with it.'

'Do they think someone else might come to a different conclusion?'

'Who knows?' Robert shrugged. 'It's like with this Costas fellow. He seems to be intent on driving the price up, too. And for what? I ask you! That place next door has been abandoned for years, and nobody else has shown any interest.'

Kate was careful with her response. 'I thought you were joking when you said you had made Mr Costas an offer. You weren't, were you?'

'Of course not.' Robert looked amused. 'Why would I joke about something like that?'

'To tease me?'

'Come here! I'm not letting you get away with that.'

Reluctantly, she allowed herself to be dragged into his embrace.

'What's wrong?' he asked suddenly, sensing her reluctance.

She shrugged. 'It's been a long, hard day for me, too, Robert. My back aches, my arm hurts, my . . . need I go on?'

'No, of course not. Let's just have a quiet evening.'

As an afterthought, Robert said, 'It's not getting too much for you, is it?'

'What?'

'The job. It's a lot of work for . . . '

'For a woman?'

'No, of course not. That's not what I meant,' he added unconvincingly. 'I meant that perhaps you would be better off doing some other kind of work.'

'Like what?'

'Oh, I don't know.' He shrugged and tossed out an idea she suspected he had been thinking of for a while. 'Come and work for me, for example. Be my personal assistant. Heaven knows I need one.'

'Doing what, may I ask?'

He laughed. 'All the things I'm not very good at. Keeping records, for example. Booking travel tickets and events. Taking minutes. Sitting in on development meetings, where we look at the designs.'

'But I like plants, Robert! That's why I've built this ridiculous little business I have. I'm a plantswoman, if there is such a word, not a glorified secretary.'

'Well, our projects often have some

planting schemes.'

'Around the edges, you mean?'

He shrugged and changed the subject, sensing he was in danger of trespassing on difficult territory. Then they opened a bottle of wine and ate their meal. It was OK, a relaxed, low-key evening, but the atmosphere wasn't the best. Conversation lagged. The gap between them seemed to yawn ever wider.

'Do you know, Robert,' Kate said at last, 'I do wish you would drop this idea of a development project at Hillside House. I really don't want you to go ahead with it.'

He smiled. 'Come on, Kate! You can't stop progress.'

'You keep saying that, but is that what it is, Robert? Really?'

'Of course it is. If I don't knock the place down, someone else will eventually.'

She wondered about that. She really did. Surely it didn't have to be like that?

'I would like to see it restored and

lived in again, not demolished,' she said.

'You've got to be realistic, Kate. Houses like that have had their day. Besides, development projects are what I do for a living.'

'Yes,' she said, nodding. 'I under-stand that.'

The she thought: how did I ever get involved with someone like Robert?

* * *

Returning from work the following day, Kate saw Mr Costas standing beneath a massive tree, a Scots Pine, close to the border with her own garden. To her astonishment, she saw that he was holding a big saw in one hand and looking speculatively up at the tree. Oh, no! she thought. Surely not?

'Mr Costas!' she called. 'Mr Costas, wait!'

He turned towards her and watched her approach.

'Mr Costas, what are you doing?' she

asked breathlessly.

'I'm going to cut down this tree, Miss Jackson.'

He lifted the saw up for her inspection and added, 'It will be difficult. All I have to do it with is this ancient saw I found in a shed. It's not much good, but I've done my best to sharpen it, and it will have to do.

'It would be better with a chainsaw,' he added wistfully. 'Then the tree is down in one minute flat. Maybe less.'

'Mr Costas,' she said carefully, 'I would prefer it if you would not cut the tree down at all.'

'You would?' He looked at her with surprise.

'It's a fine tree,' she said slowly. 'There's nothing wrong with it. It has taken many years for it to grow to this size. Maybe a hundred. More. You can't just destroy it for no good reason.'

'True,' he said, nodding, 'but a tree like this uses so much water. Do you know how many gallons it consumes in a single day?'

'No, of course not. But so what?' she said, more than a little impatiently.

'Water is a valuable resource. We can't afford to waste it. Global warming, Miss Jackson. Drought. The world faces a water shortage. Millions of people are dying because of crop failure when the rains didn't come.'

Kate shook her head now, utterly bewildered by the course of the conversation.

'Mr Costas . . . ' she began.

'Elek, please.'

'Elek,' she repeated experimentally, 'are you entirely serious, or are you just pulling my leg?'

He looked puzzled now. 'Pulling your leg?'

'Teasing.'

His face cleared. 'Miss Jackson . . . '

'Kate.'

'Kate.' He gave her a little bow in acknowledgement. 'Kate, of course I am not teasing. What do you mean?'

'Elek, this is not Africa, or a desert anywhere else in the world. We have far more water than we need or want on this hillside. There is no shortage at all here.

'We gardeners, and the farmers as well, spend half our lives digging drainage ditches to get rid of surplus water so that we can grow things on the land. This is not Kent — or Cyprus! We do not have a shortage of water in Northumberland, and saving water here is not going to help a single person in sub-Saharan Africa!'

He shrugged. 'All I know . . . ' He paused to consider what she'd just said. 'You are a gardener?'

'Of course. I have a garden. You have seen it.'

'I mean a proper one.'

'A proper one? Oh, I see what you mean. The answer is yes, of course. You have seen my truck. You have watched me going to work every day. Yes, I am a professional gardener.'

'How is this possible?' he murmured, shaking his head and suddenly wearing a big smile. 'It is wonderful. I live next to a gardener!'

'What's so unusual about that?' She bristled. 'Is it because I'm a woman? You're not used to seeing women gardeners? I've got news for you, Elek — there's lots of women gardeners in this country!'

'No, no! That's not it at all. My surprise is because I, too, am a gardener.'

As she stared at him, struggling to understand, he added, 'I am pleased you are my neighbour, Kate. Now we can talk together about gardens.

'If you wish?' he added shyly. 'Maybe you don't like to talk about your work?'

'Elek,' she said, beginning to recover, 'there is nothing I enjoy more than talking about gardens and plants. They are my life!'

11

'Tell me about your gardening,' Kate said, intrigued now.

'Well, I am from Cyprus, as I said,' Elek said, smiling. 'There, I had what I believe you would call a market garden. I grew vegetables mostly.'

'Really? How interesting. Tell me more, Mr Costas. Elek, I mean.'

'It was a good business,' Elek said with a shrug and a modest smile. 'Very good. I worked hard for ten, fifteen years. My customers were very pleased, I was very pleased, the people who worked for me . . . and so on. But now it is all gone. Bust.'

'What happened?'

'The economic crisis blew me out of the water. You have heard that in Cyprus the economy isn't very good lately?'

'Yes, sort of,' Kate frowned as she

tried to recall what she had heard. 'I gather there have been problems, but I don't really follow the news closely.'

'Especially the news from a tiny island far away?' Elek suggested with a rueful smile.

Kate chuckled, feeling slightly embarrassed. 'It's not that! It's just that we have so much news these days. All day long it pours out of TVs and radios, newspapers and mobile phones.'

'The twenty-four hour news culture, eh?'

'Exactly. And if you are trying to run and build a business, it is impossible to keep up with it all. There are only so many hours in the day, Elek.'

'I know this,' he said ruefully. 'You can't tell me anything new about this. I worked like a slave. No time for watching TV, visiting friends, sitting and drinking wine . . . Nothing! My life was my business, and my business my life.

'Then it all went kaput anyway. Suddenly I had all the time in the world, but that was worse. Free time is no good without money. They should teach that in schools. Maybe they do now. I don't know,' he added with a shrug.

'How did the collapse happen?'

'Crooks and gamblers ran our banks. One day they found they were running out of money. Nobody could find the stop tap. It was like pouring money into sand. It just disappeared.

'By the end, the government was taxing people's savings, and nobody wanted to buy anything anymore. Restaurants closed. Shops cut back on their orders. And I couldn't sell my crops, even at give-away prices.

'There was no money to pay my boys, the ones who worked for me. They say: Elek, we will work for nothing until things get better. I say no. That's no good. Take as much as you want from the garden, but the business is finished. I must do something else now. So must you. Then we had a big party, which was very sad, and I left.'

'But you still owned the land, the property?'

'No. I don't think so. The money to buy it was borrowed, and when you can no longer pay what is due each month the bank or the finance company takes it over. Isn't it the same here?'

Kate supposed it was. Somebody like Robert would move in and grab what was left. What a sad tale! It was a wonder anyone ever bothered starting a business.

'How awful, Elek.'

'It is life,' he said with a shrug. 'These things happen.'

'What did you grow, when the business was still doing well?'

Elek came back to life. 'Everything! Everything it is possible to eat: the biggest, sweetest tomatoes, the juiciest melons, lettuce, onions, potatoes . . . '

It seemed as if the list was endless, and it sounded like a lot of hard work. She could imagine the job it must have been to get vegetables to market while they were still at their best.

'So you were very labour intensive?' she suggested. 'Constant attention would have been needed to grow all those crops?'

'Oh, yes! But the big problem was always the water. My country has a problem with its water supply. There isn't enough. Sometimes people have water in their homes only every other day. Not the hotels, of course. They must keep the tourists happy, or that would be another industry bankrupt.'

'What about farms and market gardens? What happens with them?'

'We must be very careful. Water is expensive and in short supply. We have wells, but often there is nothing in them. So we have to be careful with water, and use it well. No wastage can be tolerated.'

'Which is why you chop down unnecessary trees?' Kate suggested with a smile.

'Exactly. Trees, weeds, plants that are no good to us — everything like that.'

'But not this one, I hope?' she said, nodding towards the Scots Pine that had been under threat.

Elek grinned. 'Perhaps not, now you have explained how much you like it.'

They talked for a few more minutes. Then Kate caught sight of Elek's watch and was horrified by the time.

'Sorry, Elek. I must go. I've got things to do. But it's been lovely talking to you, and most interesting. Perhaps we can do it again sometime?'

He nodded. 'Certainly. That would be good.'

Kate left him then, her head full of unasked and unanswered questions. The big one was how, in view of his financial catastrophe, Elek Costas had come to acquire the ownership of Hillside House in north Northumberland. She still didn't have a clue as to how that had come about.

Perhaps next time, Kate thought as she climbed into her truck. Of one thing she was sure, though. She would be speaking to Elek Costas again. There wasn't any doubt about that. Well, well, well! she thought. Just fancy that. I have a professional gardener for a neighbour. Who would have thought it?

12

The message awaiting her on the phone that evening caused her to step back and think again about her inquiries about Mrs Fenwick. The message was from Mr Prescott in Cheltenham. It was brief and to the point, brutally and unhelpfully so.

'Miss Jackson, just as I forecast, my client has no wish to enter into correspondence with you. Nor does she wish to speak to you or meet you. There, I have to insist, we must leave it.

'I am sorry to have been unable to help you with this matter, Miss Jackson, but my client's wishes take precedence over any other consideration, certainly so far as I am concerned.

'Good day to you, Miss Jackson.'

Pompous ass! Kate thought once again. Then she scowled and deleted the message. Were all solicitors like that? she wondered. Perhaps she should ask Graham Matthews. He certainly wasn't.

One thing was immediately and starkly clear now: she was not going to get any help at all from Mr Prescott in Cheltenham. She could drop that idea.

★   ★   ★

'Of course not, dear,' Frances said with equanimity. 'The gentleman in question — and he obviously is a gentleman — is a properly professional man. No one in such a position of trust will put a casual caller ahead of his client. It would be professional suicide.'

'I suppose it would,' Kate admitted reluctantly. 'But that thought is no help to me at all. Nor are you, Frances, if it comes to that.'

Frances sighed and said, 'I really wish you would just drop the whole subject, Kate. What does it matter? What more do you hope to discover, now that you know Mr Costas really is the owner of Hillside House?'

'I don't know, to be honest.' It was Kate's turn to sigh. 'It's just that I want to know what happened. How has Elek Costas come into possession of Hillside House? He went bankrupt in Cyprus, he told me. So how could he afford to buy such a big property here?'

'Kate, dear, is it really any of your business? Can you not just accept that you have a new neighbour, and learn to live alongside him?

'He might be rude and unfriendly — offensive even, perhaps — but he's still your neighbour. Learn to live with it, and with him.'

Kate smiled ruefully. 'You're right, Frances. Of course you are. How silly I must seem. You're such a sensible person, and I'm so lucky to have you as a friend.'

'I don't know about that. But I do know that there's no point focussing on things you can do nothing about. Life is too short.'

Kate brooded a moment and then changed the subject.

'I like that jumper you're knitting.'

'Do you really?'

'Yes. It's lovely. And how clever of you to make it big enough to wear over other things when winter comes.'

'Yes, well . . . How is Robert, by the way?'

'Oh, Robert! We're in the midst of a little spat, I'm afraid.'

'What about? It's not like you, either of you.'

'Hillside House, of course. Robert is determined to press on with his offer to Mr Costas, despite my preferences.'

'Is he now? He sees things very differently to you, then, doesn't he?'

'He does.' Kate frowned. 'Robert accuses me of failing to recognise reality — of being a Luddite even! He talks about progress, and how inevitable it is. Someone will make a lot of money eventually out of building a load of houses on that site, he says, and he wants it to be him.'

'Oh, dear.'

'What do you think, Frances?'

'About Hillside House?'

'Yes.'

Frances paused for a moment and gave the question some thought. 'To be honest, I can see Robert's point of view. We're always being told how more houses are needed to accommodate a growing population, aren't we?'

'Perhaps we are, but surely that doesn't mean we need more new houses everywhere, does it? I like Hillside House. I don't want to see it knocked down, especially by my boyfriend. I would like to see it restored, and people living in it again. Surely, that would be progress, as well?'

'Ah!' Frances paused and smiled. 'You have a point. Well, still in the mode of speaking honestly, I have to say I agree with you. I, too, like Hillside House. I should hate to see it go.

'The important question, though, is what all this means for your relationship with Robert?'

Kate shook her head. 'I don't know,' she said with a weary sigh. 'I just hope we'll get past it somehow.'

13

Robert was in a bad mood. He wasn't saying much, but she could always tell. Partly, it was precisely because he wasn't saying much. It was also because he picked at his food, food that she had diligently cooked and presented. She wished she hadn't bothered. Robert had wanted them to go out for a meal, and now she wished she had agreed. At the time, though, she had thought it would better to have an evening at home, as a way of easing whatever tension there was between them. Not that that was the reason for his poor spirits.

'You've had another tough week, I gather?' she said quietly.

He gave her a wan smile. 'You might say that. In fact, you should. It has all run away like sand through my fingers this week. I should just have taken the week off, and stayed here to help you with the garden. That would have been more productive.'

'I would have liked that,' she said with a smile. 'My garden has been getting away from me, I've been so busy with other people's. Still, that's what pays the bills. I shouldn't complain.'

'Have you finished with the Matthews' place yet?'

'Just about. There's some fine-tuning to do when the plants grow up a bit, but the other day I started another project for an old client over at Stainton.'

'Do I know him?'

'It's a her, actually. Minnie Atkins. She has a pub, and wants me to develop a beer garden for her.'

'I'm surprised she doesn't have one already.'

'Oh, she does! But it's all nettles, brambles and fag ends at the moment.'

'So what you're really saying is that she wants somewhere outside for the smokers to sit? Somewhere sheltered from the wind by attractive flowers and shrubs, and with a roof to keep the rain off and a couple of those patio heaters for when winter comes and it gets frosty.'

'How did you know?' Kate asked with mock surprise.

'I've seen them, the smokers. I've seen them up and down the country, huddled on doorsteps, hidden in doorways, sheltering their cigarettes from the wind and the rain. It's pathetic. I would often feel really sorry for them if I thought they were doing themselves any good by keeping up their ridiculous habit. Can't they see they're humiliating themselves?'

Phew! Kate thought. But at least Robert was smiling now, which was a better sign.

'I don't disagree with you,' she said. 'But have you never been a smoker?'

'Never. I was an athlete when I was at school, and I've tried to keep myself pretty fit ever since. Besides,' he added with a grin, 'it's a very expensive habit.

I never had the money!'

'Until now?'

'Not even now. What money I have now I have to spend on champagne and expensive whisky for clients.'

'A drop of which never passes your lips?'

'Never!'

She laughed.

'Anyway, Robert, Minnie Atkins has a nice little project for me. No doubt there will be smokers in the beer garden, but there will also be people with young children, and people with elderly parents who want a nice meal in pleasant surroundings. Apparently, the pub trade is mostly about food these days, rather than beer.'

'I don't think people wanting a nice meal are going to be happy about being surrounded by smokers in a beer garden, especially when the rain starts.'

'Robert, stop being so cynical! Anyway, I've thought of that. The tables will all have big umbrellas that can be put up to keep off the rain.'

'What about the smokers, though?'

'I've thought of that, as well. We'll only put ashtrays on the tables in one tucked-away section.'

'They'll just move them to where they want to be.'

Kate shook her head. 'No they won't. The ashtrays will be fixed, and immovable, and the tables without them will have 'No Smoking' signs permanently fixed as well. How am I doing?'

Robert laughed. 'You've thought of everything.'

'Not quite, but I'm getting there. The main problem is that I still need some help. But I'll find some eventually.

'By the way,' she added, 'I've spoken to my new neighbour once or twice recently. Mr Costas? He's not as bad as I thought at first. Perhaps because we have something in common.'

'What's that?' Robert asked suspiciously.

'He's a gardener, too.'

Robert shook his head and gave a

cynical little laugh, as if to say he couldn't believe it.

'He is! He's from Cyprus, where he tells me he had a market garden until he went bankrupt. He lost the lot, apparently. Everything. He says the economy over there has been a bit shaky.'

'I'll say!' Robert chuckled. 'It was front-page news every day for a while, even here. The EU — Germany, mostly, through the Eurozone — had to bail them out.

'Still,' he reflected, 'it's an ill wind that blows no good, isn't it?'

'Is it?'

'Well, if Costas went bust, he must be in need of cash. He'll be desperate. I'm glad you've told me this, Kate. It should make him easier to deal with.'

She looked up uncertainly. 'You are joking, aren't you?'

'Not at all!' Robert shook his head. 'It's the situation you dream about when you're negotiating with someone. The more desperate they are, the easier it is to beat them down.'

'He's a really nice man, Robert!'

'This is business, sweetheart. You can't afford emotional sympathy in business. You'd soon end up in the bankruptcy court.'

'He's a nice man,' she repeated, 'and he's obviously had a lot of difficulties. To have uprooted and come here . . . He needs help and support, Robert, not someone taking advantage of him.'

Robert gave a nasty-sounding short little laugh and went to pour himself a glass of water from the kitchen tap.

Kate stared after him. She was stunned. She couldn't believe how he was looking at it. What on earth was wrong with him? She bitterly regretted saying what she had said about Elek now.

'That's really not a good way to look at things, Robert,' she said, striving to keep her tone even. 'He's my neighbour and I like him.'

Robert laughed again. 'It is, as far as I'm concerned! It should make it easier to persuade him to sell Hillside House. Mind you, he hasn't come back on my offer yet. I don't know what's holding him up, especially if he's got no money.'

'Maybe he doesn't want to sell? Maybe he likes the house?'

'Maybe.' Robert looked at her suspiciously. 'I hope you haven't been pouring your eccentric ideas into his ear, Kate.'

'Whatever do you mean?'

'You know perfectly well what I mean. You've told me more than once how you feel about that decrepit slum next door. Don't you go telling Costas it's an architectural treasure that ought to be saved for the nation.

'It's all right being sentimental, but let's get real here. That place needs to come down. A site like that is ripe for redevelopment. I'm not having you interfering and making my job even more difficult.

'It's time for some blunt speaking,' he added, just in case she hadn't got the message yet.

Her heart skipped a beat. Two, in

121

fact. And it was with tension, not pleasure. She couldn't believe what she was hearing. This had become more than silly. It was on the borders of outrageous and disgusting.

'Robert!'

He glared at her.

'Robert, how dare you speak to me like that?'

'Because I'm telling you like it is. You're being stubborn and silly about a heap of old junk. To repeat, I do not want you to interfere and slow down or stop this project I'm trying to get off the ground.

'Hillside House is going to give us the financial base for everything else in our lives. And it's going to happen. I promise you that!'

She stared back at him a moment, and shook her head. Then she got up and began clearing the table, working hard to stay calm. Things had got out of hand.

Robert must have realised the same thing. He got up and wrapped his arms around her. She shrugged him off.

'Come on, Kate! Don't be like that.'

She spun round to face him and said coolly, 'I think you'd better go, Robert. You've said quite enough for one night. I'm not having any man speaking to me like that in my own home, not even you. Not now, and not in the future either.

'And before you go, let me just tell you there's no need for you to be planning a joint financial future for us — or any other kind of joint future either. Our relationship hasn't got that far, and I'm not sure now that it ever will.'

'I didn't mean . . . ' he began.

'Go, Robert. Just go!'

She turned back to the kitchen sink and began to run hot water over the dishes. She squeezed in some washing-up liquid and watched the soap suds form beautiful bubbles with a sort of bluish-yellow tint to them.

When she heard the front door slam shut, a tear escaped to roll unhindered down her cheek.

14

At that time of year, late April, the sun rose at about 5.30 in the morning. Then there often followed many hours of sunshine before the usual mid-day clouds built up, so the mornings were lovely, with good growing weather — and without the midges that tended to come out in the evenings later on in the summer. Kate tried to make the most of them, often doing some work in her own garden for an hour or two before setting off to see whichever client she was working for at the time. Otherwise, as she said to Frances, she might as well not have had a garden of her own. She had so little time to tend it.

After her epic row with Robert she found sleep difficult to come by, and was glad when early morning sunshine brought the night to an end. By six, she was outside, sowing seeds and planting onion sets in her vegetable garden, getting ready for the new growing season.

It was a beautiful new day, the air still cool, but the sun promised to warm things up rapidly. She enjoyed the thrill of planting and sowing, and for a time she was able to forget about the unpleasantness of the previous evening, and the long night that had followed. Gardening could bring its own rewards to even the most tortured soul.

'You're making an early start, I see.'

She jumped and spun round. 'Elek! You startled me.'

He was watching her from a gap in the hedge between their respective gardens. Now he smiled apologetically. 'I am sorry, Kate. I thought you had seen me.'

'Well, I hadn't, and I didn't expect to see anyone for hours yet. No one gets up this early, except me.'

He shrugged. 'Always I am up by this time. All my life. It is the best time, before it gets too hot.'

She chuckled. 'No fear of that here, Elek! This is Northumberland. We never get too hot here.'

He nodded agreement. 'I am discovering that already. This is very cold country. No good for my tomatoes. I have planted the seeds, but I don't know what will happen. Maybe nothing.'

'Tomatoes? Don't tell me you have planted them outdoors?'

'Of course. Where else would I put them?'

She chuckled. 'Oh, Elek! You'll be very lucky indeed to grow tomatoes outdoors here, unless they're the little cherry tomatoes on a bush plant. In a good summer they can do quite well. But otherwise ... Well, you need a greenhouse or a poly tunnel for growing ordinary tomatoes.'

Elek nodded again, as if resigned now to the failure of his tomato crop. 'So what are you planting?' he asked.

'Onions and potatoes at the moment.

Later, I'll put in some salad crops. Runner beans as well, probably, and peas. Standard vegetables like that. They should do all right, if we have anything like a decent summer.'

'Need any help?'

'No, it's all right, thanks. I'm just doing a bit of sowing and planting before I go to work.'

Elek shivered and looked desolate. 'It's too cold here for gardening. I've cleared some ground ready for planting, but maybe I won't bother. Nothing will grow, I think.'

'Of course it will!' She laughed and added, 'Just don't think you can grow tropical fruits outdoors in Northumberland!'

'I can see that.' He shook his head wistfully. 'I can see what it is like here. Only flowers. People grow only flowers.'

'That's because they like floral gardens, not because it's all they can grow.'

'But people must eat. It can't be only flowers. You grow potatoes, though.

That's good. What kind are they?'

'Those I've just put in are what we call 'first earlies'.'

Elek looked puzzled. 'I don't know this one. First earlies? That is their name?'

'No, no! 'Pentland Javelin' is their name. They're amongst the first of the new potatoes. Then we have second earlies. Both categories grow faster and mature a little earlier than the maincrop varieties.'

Elek looked astonished. 'In Cyprus we don't have such things. We just grow potatoes, and we have four crops a year.'

'Four crops a year?' Kate repeated, astonished.

'Yes. It is normal. We harvest four crops in one year.'

'That's amazing, Elek. I didn't know that was possible. How wonderful!'

He shrugged. 'It is normal there. But here,' he added, with a disparaging wave at the still cold ground, 'maybe no crop in a year. The seed potatoes will just rot in the ground, I think. Maybe I should go home now — sell my house and go back there.'

Kate didn't know what to say. He looked and sounded so desolate.

But suddenly he beamed at her, chuckled and said, 'Then you will no longer have a difficult neighbour!'

She laughed and waved the suggestion aside. They continued talking about gardens and plants for a while. Then Kate returned apprehensively to the subject that had tormented her half the night.

'Elek, are you really thinking of selling Hillside House? Will you accept Robert's offer, do you think?'

'I don't know. Maybe. He wants my house pretty badly. He keeps phoning me about it.'

Kate rammed the spade hard into the ground, trying not to give away how she felt.

'I don't know why he wants it,' Elek added. 'Do you know?'

She shrugged. 'He thinks he can

make money out of it. That's what he does — property deals. He's a developer.'

Elek shrugged. 'He wants to pull my house down, I think. Maybe he thinks it is one of those things that make your eyes hurt?'

She laughed. 'Oh, Elek! What things?'

He mimed pain in one eye, closing it up and grimacing, pressing a hand to his face. 'Oh! An eyesore? Is that what you mean?' she said, shaking her head and laughing again.

'Exactly.' He nodded. 'Eyesore. Is that how Robert thinks about my house?'

'Something like that, I think. And you're right. He does want to pull it down. Then he would build new houses on the site. That's the general idea, anyway.'

Elek mulled it over for a moment and then said, 'What about you, Kate? Is that how you feel about my house, too?'

'No, Elek. Not at all. I think it's a lovely old house. I would like to see it restored, not demolished. I would like to see the garden restored, too, not concreted over and houses built on it.'

'Then you must speak to your boyfriend.'

'I have done. I've made my position quite clear to him, not that it seems to make any difference.'

Elek looked solemn for a few moments. Then his wonderful smile reappeared.

'On second thoughts, Kate, let Robert buy it and pull it down. Then I can go home with the money he pays me, and live in sunshine all the days of my life.'

'But without enough water,' she pointed out, responding to his good humour.

He grimaced at the thought. 'Maybe not, then,' he conceded. 'Maybe I will keep it, and stay here.'

She finished raking a thin cover of soil over the seeds she had planted and straightened up. 'Come on, Elek,' she said, turning to him with a smile. 'I've still got a little time left before I must go to work. Show me what you've been doing in your garden.'

15

Kate couldn't believe how much ground Elek had cleared. Vast patches of bramble had been torn out and piled into mountainous heaps. Dead trees and shrubs had been felled and sawn into logs. Bracken had been cut, trampled and dug out. Rectangles of bare earth could now be seen in several places, where the soil had been turned with a spade.

'Elek,' she said with wonder and delight, 'you're creating a farm!'

'No, no. Just tidying up, and maybe growing some vegetables.'

'I can't believe you've done so much work — and without me noticing, too!'

'I get up early,' he said with a shrug, 'and I have nothing else to do.'

'Even so . . . ' Thoughts were suddenly buzzing in her head. What if . . . ? No, no. It was too soon to be asking if he needed any help.

'Have you planted any potatoes?' she asked instead.

'Some,' he admitted. 'Maybe they will be ready in two or three years' time in this cold soil.'

She laughed. 'What a pessimist you are! By late July or early August, you will have some potatoes ready, I promise you. And what have we here?' she added, turning to a bed that had obviously been newly sown.

'Sunflowers,' he said with a shrug. 'Sunflower seeds are very useful. I like to eat them. So do birds, unfortunately.'

'Sunflower seeds? Maybe not here, Elek. But you never know. You could be lucky. We might have a good summer this year.'

'Yes?'

He seemed doubtful about the prospects for the summer, but not too despondent. In fact, he was suddenly energetic and enthusiastic as he showed her around the garden. She sensed that he was happy to have someone taking an interest, especially an informed interest, and she guessed he had been having rather a lonely time.

'There's an awful lot of waste to get rid of,' she said, looking round at the heaps of material his land-clearing had generated. 'I hope you're not thinking of burning it? We're not supposed to have bonfires in this country now, you know, because of the air pollution they cause.'

He shrugged. 'I haven't got that far. I don't know what I will do with it.'

'Well, some you can compost. That will give you wonderful material to add to the soil. I've got an industrial shredder we could use to break the stuff down first. You're welcome to use that.'

She gazed around and added, 'Then all that wood . . . '

'Maybe for the fire in the house?'

'Yes. Or a wood-burning stove, like mine, which you could tie in to the heating system. Anyway, for now just cut it and stack it.'

'It will take a long time to cut it,' he

said with regret. 'The saw is old, and not very sharp.'

'Get a new one! Better yet, borrow my chainsaw.'

It suddenly struck her that he might not have the money to buy a new saw. After all, he didn't seem to have any sort of vehicle. Was it possible that he had a big, old house but no money to go with it? Perhaps Robert was right, and Elek was in no position to negotiate. Trust Robert!

Then a new thought came to her. She paused and looked at Elek thoughtfully. 'Elek, you've done so much work here. You're not really thinking of selling to Robert, are you?'

'It is a very good offer,' he said with a shrug. 'With the money . . . '

'Elek?'

They stared at each other for a moment. Then a sheepish smile spread across his face. 'No,' he admitted, shaking his head. 'I think not. At least, I don't want to. Maybe I can do something good here.'

'Like restore the garden, perhaps?'

'And the house.'

'Really? Oh, Elek! That's wonderful news, if you're thinking like that.'

It was hard at that moment to keep from hugging him with delight. Somehow she managed it.

'I've never been inside the house,' she added. 'What's it like inside? Is it in poor condition?'

He shrugged. 'It needs some work, I think.'

'So it would take a lot of money?'

'Not really. Some money, yes, but I can do such work myself.'

'You can?'

'Not everything, of course, but most of it, over time.'

'You'll need help with things like the electrics, of course.'

'No, I don't think so. I can do electrics myself.'

'No, Elek. You won't be qualified to do such work, are you?'

He chuckled. 'Not qualified maybe — but I can do the job.'

'That's not the point, Elek. In this country you need special qualifications for such work to be legal.'

Elek held up his hands in a gesture of surrender. 'OK. I will get qualifications.'

'That could take a long time. Years even. Better to employ a qualified electrician, if you're thinking of re-wiring the house, for example. Maybe a qualified plumber, too?'

'Maybe. But to do all that would take much money.'

'Money you don't have, perhaps?' she asked, taking a gamble, hoping he wouldn't be offended.

Elek nodded. 'Not now, no.'

So there it was: the opening she had suspected might appear if she were patient enough.

'Elek,' she said slowly, 'would you like to come to my house and have coffee with me?'

'When?' he asked with surprise.

'Now, Elek. Right now! I have a proposition to put to you.'

16

'Nice house,' Elek said, looking round the kitchen appreciatively.

'Thank you, Elek. Now sit down here while I make some coffee. Then I have something to ask you.'

'Just ask me now.'

'It can wait a minute.'

She wasn't sure quite how to phrase the question she wanted to ask. It was so difficult to know how an invitation from her, a proposal if you like, would be received. But there was no question in her mind: she was going to do it. Elek just might be the person she had been seeking for so long.

'It's wonderful,' she said slowly, 'to be able to talk to you about gardening and plants, and everything. You are a fellow professional, a true colleague, Elek!'

'It is true,' he admitted. 'At least, I used to be a professional gardener, for many, many years. Not now though, unfortunately.' He shrugged and added, 'But, yes, I know what you mean. It is only since I started digging again that I have felt at home here — and now I have you to talk to about it!'

He beamed at her.

'Kindred spirits!' she said, laughing.

She turned her attention to setting out the cups and the spoons, the milk jug and the coffee. She was trying to be careful and cautious, not to go too fast. She wanted him relaxed and unsuspecting, even though she herself was on edge.

'Elek,' she said, sitting down at last and pouring the coffee, 'do you have any money?'

'Not much,' he admitted. 'Why? Do you need some?'

He gazed at her with confusion as she covered her mouth with her hand and began to laugh. 'Oh, Elek! I'm so sorry. I didn't mean to say that. It just came out. I do apologise. Honestly! Whatever is the matter with me?'

'It's all right,' he assured her. 'If you

need a small amount of money, I can let you have it. For a bigger amount . . . ' He grinned and said, 'Maybe you should ask your boyfriend!'

'Oh, no! That wouldn't do at all. I'll start again,' Kate said with a smile, 'and try not to trip over my tongue this time.

'Elek, you know I have a gardening business, don't you?'

'Of course. I see you leave every day, in your truck with the painted signs on the side. You have told me things. So, yes, I know.'

'What I do,' she said, furrowing her brow with thought, trying to get it right, 'is I prepare garden designs for people. Then, if they like the design, I do the work to make the plan actually happen on the ground. I make the garden.'

'I understand,' Elek said, nodding. 'It is very nice to make a living this way. But maybe not much money, eh?'

'Oh, I wouldn't say that! I make enough money doing it. Not enough for Robert, maybe, but enough for some-one like me. It's a good life.'

He nodded vigorously. 'Very good, I think. So why do you want to borrow some money from me?'

'I don't! I gave you the wrong impression, Elek. Please, let me continue. This is a very busy time for me. I have a number of clients queuing up at my door. They all want a lot of work doing — and doing quickly, if not sooner! — and there's only one of me to do it. I need help with the work, but so far I haven't been able to find anyone suitable. And, believe me, I've been looking for a long time.

'Anyway, I'm about to start a big project, one that will really stretch me. It involves a lot of heavy, physical work — digging and laying patio slabs — that sort of thing — as well as tree and shrub planting. I wondered if you might be interested in helping?'

Elek stared at her, seemingly too surprised to respond immediately. She supposed she had rather thrown it at him, but she pressed on regardless.

'You're an experienced man in this

business, Elek, and I've seen how hard you can work. If you need a job, or if you're a bit short of money to help pay for improvements to Hillside House, I was thinking we might be able to help each other.'

Elek shrugged. He seemed over-whelmed.

'What I'd like to suggest is that you come with me for a day. You could see what I do, and what the job is, and you could consider if you'd like to try working with me for a few days on a trial basis. What do you think?'

Elek seemed stunned still, as well he might be, she admitted to herself. It was a lot to pitch suddenly at him from out of the blue. She watched anxiously as he considered her offer. Then she realised she had missed something important out.

'I would pay you, of course,' she said hastily. 'I would pay you a good wage for your trouble. That might help with your plans for Hillside House?'

Elek suddenly smiled. 'Kate, I would

love to help you for a few days. But are you sure I would be much use to you?'

'Most definitely. I have seen the work you've done at Hillside House, and I'm amazed by how much you've accomplished already. You're just what I need!'

He shrugged the compliment aside. 'It is nothing. I am used to such work. All my life I have worked like that. I know no different.'

'I realise that. It's what made me think of asking you in the first place. I know it would be a distraction from your own plans, but perhaps it would suit you for a time?'

'Tomorrow,' he said with a firm nod. 'I will come with you tomorrow, Kate.'

'Oh, good! Thank you, Elek. That's wonderful news.'

He grinned and sipped his coffee. 'So maybe we are no longer enemies?'

'Of course not!' Kate said, colouring with embarrassment.

'Friends and neighbours now?'

'Absolutely!' she said, laughing.

17

The job was a big one. She had agreed to take it on, but she had reservations about how long it would take her. In bad moments, she could see herself still working on it next year, not just for the next month or two. In weak, realistic moments, she had even contemplated owning up and saying it was too much for her. That, of course, would have ruled her out of a lot of other work, as well as this project, as word would have spread and people would shake their heads and express doubts about her capabilities.

'Where are we going?' Elek asked as she got the truck moving the morning the project was to start.

'Fawdon, a village about ten miles away. Do you know the area?'

He shook his head. 'I know only

where the post office is and the grocery store.'

'In Fawdon?'

'No. In this village, Callerton. As for the rest of it,' he added, waving to take in the remainder of Northumberland, 'I know nothing.'

She chuckled. 'Well, Callerton is unusual these days in that it has a few shops. Fawdon doesn't have any at all. But it's a nice, sleepy little place.'

'We will wake it up, perhaps.'

'Not today, we won't. Today I want just to show you what there is to do, and maybe make a start on clearing up and doing some measuring. Then you can let me know if you're interested in continuing to work with me.'

'Will it be cold there?'

'In Fawdon? Not really, no. No different to Callerton. It's not that far away.'

'Then it will be cold,' Elek said, shivering in anticipation.

She winced. She hadn't thought of that. Elek was used to warm weather.

Hot weather, even. Perhaps she had made a mistake in inviting him along? She hoped not. She didn't want someone who wasn't weatherproof. That would be no good when the nights closed in and the cold wind began to blow. But perhaps Elek would be long gone by then anyway.

'But I am prepared,' Elek added.

She glanced round and noted his sweater and heavy jacket. He pulled gloves out of one pocket and a woolly hat out of another, giving her even more cause for concern.

'It won't be that bad,' she said. 'Oh, dear. It didn't occur to me that it might be too cold for you.'

'It's all right,' he assured her. 'Really. I found this in the house.'

He opened the canvas sack he had brought with him and pulled out something heavy. She stared hard, so astonished that for a moment she forgot she was the driver and almost ran them off the road. Elek looked at her and grinned.

'Oh, Elek!' She began to laugh riotously. 'Wherever did you find that?'

He was holding up an old-fashioned pot hot-water bottle, wrapped in a knitted woollen cover.

'Under a bed,' said Elek, shrugging. 'I had no idea what it was for. So I looked on the internet to see what it was. It's a . . .'

'I know perfectly well what it is, Elek. My granny had one.' She laughed and added, 'You're a regular joker, aren't you? We should have some fun today.'

★　★　★

The job was at Linden Cottage, a pretty little Victorian cottage that had been long neglected until bought a year earlier by a woman who wrote children's stories, and who had fled London to write more of them in peace. Too many distractions in London, she had said. Well, Kate had replied, you'll find none at all here.

Now the renovations to the cottage

147

itself were complete and attention had turned to the garden, which was extensive, and for which the owner had ambitious expectations that Kate hoped she would be able to match. She decided to take Elek on a tour of the site as soon as they arrived and explain to him what the owner, Miss Carrington, wanted.

'Nice place,' Elek remarked as they drew up outside the cottage.

'It is now, but a year ago you might not have said that. The builders have done wonders. Now it's my turn. I don't believe anyone has done any gardening here for half a century. So it's a big challenge.'

Elek shook his head and muttered about how unsurprising that was, given how cold it was here.

'Oh, shut up, Elek! Cold? This is summer.'

He grinned and followed her out of the cab. Miss Carrington was waiting for them at the gate.

'Good morning, Kate! Nice to see

you so bright and early.'

'Good morning!' Kate called back. 'Miss Carrington, this is my friend and colleague, Elek. I'm going to show him round your garden, if you don't mind, and then we'll do a bit of preparatory work. Nothing involving machinery this morning, though, if you're worried about the noise level.'

'You can make as much noise as you like, dear. I'm on my way out for the day. You've only just caught me. I'm going into town. That is, assuming you don't need me here for any reason?'

'No. You go right ahead. Have a lovely day.'

'Elek?' Miss Carrington said thoughtfully, turning to Kate's companion. 'Is that a Celtic name?'

'I believe so,' Elek said agreeably.

'How interesting.'

'Elek is from Cyprus,' Kate said firmly, fearing the conversation might get out of hand.

'Ah!' Miss Carrington smiled, her

eyes sparkling, and said, 'Greek Celtic, then?'

'Exactly,' Elek said with his most charming smile.

Greek Celtic indeed! Kate thought with despair. They were as bad as one another.

★　★　★

Miss Carrington departed and Kate began the tour. She dealt with it objectively, wanting Elek to get a good idea of what the gardener's life here was like.

'Sometimes,' she said briskly, 'we have long winters in Northumberland. Not always, but the last few have lasted from November through to late April. We can have frost even in May, although the early sun soon melts it by that time of year.

'Summers are not as hot as you are used to, Elek, but we do have the advantage — so far as plants are concerned — of plenty of rain. Water,' she added with a meaningful look, 'is not a problem here.'

'So we don't cut down any more trees?' he said, looking disappointed for a moment before giving her a big grin.

Kate smiled, shook her head and opened the gate leading into the garden. When she turned round to speak to Elek, he was crouched down, his fingers probing at something on the ground.

'What are you doing?'

'Testing the soil.'

He straightened up and studied the handful of earth he had gathered. 'Not good,' he pronounced with a grimace, his fingers riffling through the soil sample.

'Not great, no. But good enough. We do have some wonderful gardens in Northumberland.'

'Probably acid,' Elek said, his fingers still working.

'Yes, you're right. The soils are generally acid. Farmers have always had to apply plenty of lime to their land in this part of the country. In the olden days there were lime kilns all over the place, to make the lime they needed for the farmland.'

She was impressed that he had seized on the character of the soil so quickly. It seemed a very professional thing to have done. But that's what he was, she reminded herself. He was a man used to growing things, and one who knew what it took to do just that. They stood together at the back of the cottage and Kate began to explain the plan.

'Miss Carrington wants a productive garden, as well as a beautiful one. So there will be herbaceous beds close to the house, but beyond them she wants a vegetable garden and a fruit orchard.

'I won't bring in plants and trees until we have the garden turned over and sectioned off, but we will need plenty of everything. There's a lot of ground to cover.'

Elek nodded thoughtfully. 'She must be a rich lady?' he suggested.

'She certainly seems to be. But don't get any ideas, Elek. You're working for me!'

He laughed aloud and shook his head.

Then she showed him a rough sketch of her ideas for the garden. He studied it and then pronounced, 'It is a good plan, I think.'

'Oh, you think so, do you? I'm so glad you approve, Elek, because actually so does Miss Carrington.'

The sarcasm was wasted. He nodded and looked up, his eyes starting to range over a garden that was very like his own at Hillside House, in its unkempt, overgrown, long-neglected state.

'So where do we start?' he asked.

'I hoped you'd say that,' Kate said, chuckling. 'Anywhere you fancy! Seriously, do you really want to be involved?'

'Of course. I am prepared for work.'

'Well, we'd better unload some tools from the truck in that case.'

Elek took off his jacket and rolled up his sleeves. Then he tightened his belt, grabbed a spade and got going. It was a good start, Kate thought with amusement, and with not a little relief.

18

At first, after their fierce argument, Kate had been so angry she had consigned Robert to oblivion, not wanting to see him ever again. It was quite possible, she knew, that he had no wish to see her again either. Common sense, or a sense of proportion, had come into play eventually, though, and they had patched things up.

So they had had an argument? So what? It had happened, but it didn't mean everything had to come to an end, Kate decided. No long-term relationship could expect to be totally free of occasional disagreement. Sensible people found ways of getting past the problem, and surely she and Robert were just that — sensible people? She certainly hoped and believed so.

So they patched things up and tried to carry on, but their relationship was not the same now. Each of them had a grievance against the other, and it showed. Kate had hoped, and assumed, that their spat had been a one-off from which they would recover eventually. But something was missing now. They seemed to be fencing around each other, on guard all the time, their easy intimacy gone. She even wondered if they should just call it a day, but that was a difficult thing to think.

She veered away from the big decision every time it came to her. She would think: Give it some time, more time. They both had a lot invested in the relationship, whatever the current difficulties. They just needed a little time, perhaps, even some time apart to allow hostilities to die down. Hopefully, then, things would be how they used to be.

'Meet me in town?' Robert suggested when he phoned next. 'I'll treat you to an expensive meal. I've had a good week.'

'Oh? Champagne and oysters?'

'Whatever is your heart's desire, my sweet.'

She laughed. 'When? And don't say tonight. I'm exhausted.'

'Tomorrow, then. Tough day gardening?'

'Very. But at least I was outdoors. So I feel healthily tired.'

'Lucky you. But at least I no longer work in smoke-filled rooms. That's a help. Seen anything of your neighbour, by the way?'

'Elek Costas? Yes. Quite a lot, actually. I've decided he's all right, is Elek. We get on fine these days.

'He's been helping me, actually. I have a big job on over at Fawdon, and as you know it's been difficult to find anyone suitable to work with me. But Elek has stepped into the breach and given me a hand.'

There followed a pause, one that stretched on a bit too long. The silence vibrated with tension.

'Robert?'

'Are you telling me that Costas has

been doing some work for you? And you are paying him, presumably?'

'Yes, of course,' she said, puzzled. 'I just told you he was working with me. Of course I'm paying him. Nobody works for nothing these days, Robert.'

'I can't believe what I'm hearing. Kate, I'm still waiting for him to get back to me about my offer for Hillside House. And you're employing him to do some gardening?'

'He's good, Robert! He's a professional horticulturist. That's what he was in Cyprus, at least. Besides, I like him, and I needed some help.'

'Don't you realise you're undermining my position? You're paying him, and giving him something interesting to do, when all I want is for him to get sick to death of the place and be desperate to sell and get out?'

Kate said nothing for a moment. Her heart started thumping. Robert's anger was something to behold. She waited for another flurry of angry criticism from him.

'Forget about dinner tomorrow,' he said wearily. 'In fact, forget about everything. You're not on my side at all, are you?'

'No, Robert. On this subject, I'm not. I've told you repeatedly how I feel about Hillside House and your proposal. I want you to forget it, and move on.'

'That's not going to happen.'

'No? Well, nothing more is going to happen between us either. We'd better call it a day.'

'Gladly. Goodbye.'

'Goodbye, Robert. Have a nice life!' she added, determined to have the last word.

* * *

Afterwards, she wondered what on earth had got into her. What had she done? That final nasty exchange was not like her at all. Robert was her partner, for goodness' sake. They were practically engaged to be married!

Well, not anymore.

Trying to stay composed, she ran the cold tap and poured herself a glass of water. Then she stood and stared despondently out of the kitchen window. All that time invested. All gone. And for what? A moment of pique.

No, she thought firmly. That wasn't it at all. There were serious differences between herself and Robert that had only just come to light. Probably they had always been there. She just hadn't acknowledged them, hadn't wanted to recognise them. It had taken this tussle over Hillside House to finally bring them out into the open.

Robert was a sophisticated, lovely man in many ways. She had been proud to have him interested in her, but . . . But? Well, he was so mercenary, for a start. His world was high finance, money and development projects. He lived and breathed property development. That was all he was really interested in, if the truth be told. What on earth would life have been like for her if they had gone on to another stage in their relationship? Miserable, probably.

No, there was no dodging the issue. He wasn't the one for her, and she wasn't the right one for him either. Why on earth hadn't they realised that a lot earlier?

She shrugged. She had rationalised things. Her thinking made sense. But she was still upset and miserable. The wounds were very raw. Salving them would take time.

* * *

She slipped on a light jacket and went off to see Frances, whom she hadn't seen for a week or so.

To her surprise, she met Elek coming out of Frances's front gate.

'Hi, Kate!' he said with his usual bright smile.

'Elek! What are you doing here?'

'The old lady, Miss Murray, asked

me if I would help her in the garden a bit. I've just been to cut the grass for her.'

'That's good of you. I know she has trouble manoeuvring the lawnmower these days, but she's always so fiercely independent that I daren't suggest I do it for her. But why didn't you tell me what you were going to do this evening?'

Elek shrugged. 'Her back is troubling her. So she asked me if I could help. Miss Murray is your friend?'

'Oh, yes! We're good friends. Normally, I pop in to see her most days, but we've been so busy this week, haven't we?'

Elek nodded and opened wide the gate for her. Kate stepped through.

'She's a nice lady,' he said. 'I like her.'

'Oh, she's been charming you, has she?'

'Home-made cake and a cup of tea!'

'Oh? You are honoured. But perhaps it was you charming her?'

He grinned and shook his head.

'Well, I'll be on my way,' he added.

'Do you still want me to help you tomorrow?'

'Yes, please! If you can spare the time?'

'No problem — like they say on TV!' Kate laughed and waved good-bye.

The brief encounter had done much to restore her spirits. It was usually like that with Elek, she had found. He was good fun, in his rather odd, endearing way. She was always glad of his company. Somehow he made the day seem brighter, and the troubles both fewer and smaller.

★   ★   ★

Frances was stuffing things in her washing machine when Kate called hello and stepped inside.

'Can I help?'

'Oh, no thank you, Kate! I can manage.'

Frances was bent double, seemingly untroubled now by any physical ailment.

163

'Is your back better?' Kate asked.

'My back?' Frances finished loading the machine and straightened up. 'My back is no worse than my front or my side, my dear. Old age hits you from every direction when it comes.'

Kate laughed. 'In that case,' she said, 'don't think you're going to steal my right-hand man away from me. If you don't really need him, you can't have him!'

Frances looked momentarily puzzled. Then she chuckled. 'You've been talking to Elek, have you?'

'I just bumped into him. He said he'd been to mow your lawn.'

'Yes, he had. He's a lovely man, isn't he? I'm so grateful to him. Come on inside. I'll make a fresh pot of tea.'

* * *

Kate brought Frances up to date on her activities, including the recruitment of Elek.

'He said he'd been doing a bit of

work for you,' Frances admitted.

'A bit? Oh, much more than that, Frances. I wouldn't have been able to handle that last job without him. I think I would have had to turn Miss Carrington down.'

'So he's a good worker?'

'Absolutely terrific! He has a lovely personality, too, when you get to know him. And he works like a Trojan. He did things easily that would have taken me forever, if I'd been able to do them at all. He knows what he's doing, as well, having been a professional gardener all his life. Did he tell you he had a market garden at home in Cyprus?'

'Yes, I believe he did,' Frances said vaguely. 'Something like that, anyway.'

'Sadly, he lost it in the economic troubles they had there recently. I feel very sorry for him. But his loss is my gain!'

Frances laughed and then said, 'I'm so glad, Kate, that you gave up your investigation into how poor Mr Costas came to own Hillside House. I thought it would all settle down if only you'd let it.'

Kate shrugged and smiled noncommittally.

'I feared it was consuming you, dear, and to no good purpose. It was really nothing to do with any of us, however curious we were. Now we've discovered he's an agreeable man and a good neighbour, after all, we can all get on with our lives, can't we?'

'Yes, I suppose so,' Kate said, thinking that perhaps now she knew him a little better she could just come out with it and ask Elek for an explanation.

'And how is Robert?'

Kate grimaced and shrugged. 'Robert is very well, I should imagine. But he and I aren't an item anymore. We've decided to split up.'

'Oh, dear! I'm so sorry, Kate.'

Kate sighed and rattled her empty tea cup. 'Is there any more tea?'

'Help yourself, dear. Pour me another one, too, if you don't mind.'

'Finishing with Robert was a good thing, you know,' Kate added, standing up to reach for the teapot. 'I'm not really unhappy about it.'

'Oh?'

'I'd come to realise recently that we were not all that well suited to each other after all. Milk?'

'Yes, please. Just a little.'

'The thing is, we don't have much in common really. Robert's driving on to be a millionaire, with his property deals, and all I want to be is a gardener. I can make a decent living out of it, and I'm happy doing it. I just love working with plants and gardens. It's all I've ever wanted to do.'

'Well, you know what they say, don't you?'

'What?'

'As one door shuts, another opens. You're still young, dear.'

Kate stared for a moment in disbelief and then she chuckled. 'Is that like saying there's plenty more fish in the sea?'

'Exactly.'

'You're a wicked lady, Frances Murray!'

'Oh, I am,' Frances said, grinning. 'You don't know the half of it either.'

19

Elek was waiting for her along the road when she left Frances's cottage. At least, he seemed to be.

'Still here, Elek?'

'Oh, I've been for a little walk,' he said awkwardly. 'I've just come back. I wasn't waiting for you.'

'It's a lovely evening, isn't it? So what are you up to now?'

'Well, I did some work in my garden. Then I stopped. Those little flying insects were bothering me.'

'Flying insects? Mosquitoes?'

'No, not mosquitoes. I know them. These are much smaller.'

'Oh, you mean midges! Yes, they can be a problem at this time of year, when there's no wind to keep them down. They're even worse in Scotland. The Isle of Skye is the worst place in the world for them.'

'Midges?' he repeated thoughtfully. 'I hate them!'

She laughed and made another little joke. Then they turned to walk along the road towards their respective homes.

'I don't know what to do inside the house,' Elek said suddenly.

'What do you mean?'

He shrugged. 'I clean up OK. No problem. But there is much work to do, I think. Repairs, and so on. Painting, perhaps. New things needed.'

'Are you saying it needs some tender loving care after all these years? Some tlc is required?'

'That's it!' Elek said, chuckling as he worked out the abbreviation. 'Exactly. Tender loving care. My house needs much of it.'

'Be patient,' she advised. 'Just do a bit at a time. Don't exhaust yourself.'

He nodded. She thought that the fact that he was thinking along those lines was good. It meant that he really wasn't going to sell to Robert. Instead, he was going to stay, hopefully. Her spirits lifted. Rats to you, Robert! she thought happily. You're not going to win this one.

'Do you know my house?' Elek asked suddenly.

'No. Like I said, I've never been inside.'

'Would you like to come and look round?'

'I'd love to, Elek. When?'

'Now is good,' he said with a smile.

★   ★   ★

The house was smaller inside than she had expected. It was more a comfortable family home than a stately mansion; one with fine views out across the valley from the main rooms, but not an absolutely enormous house. In estate agent's parlance, she could see that it could do with some 'updating', but it wasn't falling apart. Far from it. It just needed someone to live in it and freshen it up.

'Perhaps a new kitchen and bathroom?' she suggested.

'You think so?'

'Well, I would want a shower, for example, and a new bath. And in the kitchen I would want a decent modern oven and better lighting. Things like that. What about the heating system? What's that like?'

There were big, ugly radiators in every room, but they were not working at the moment.

'I don't know,' Elek admitted with a shrug.

'What kind of boiler is there?'

Elek shrugged again. 'It burns oil, I think. There's a big tank outside. But I haven't used it.'

'Not at all? Heavens, Elek! You must have been freezing at times. It's all right now, but in the spring we were still getting frost.'

'If it is cold,' he said with a grin, 'I get up earlier and work faster in the garden.'

She laughed, but she suspected he meant it.

'Still,' she said, still fishing, 'none of

this would matter if you were going to sell to Robert, would it? Are you one hundred percent sure now that you are not?'

Elek laughed. 'One hundred per cent!' he agreed.

'Your boyfriend is a strange man,' he added, shaking his head. 'It is not reasonable to buy such a house and then pull it down.'

'I agree. I like this old place. It should be restored and lived in, not pulled down. Besides, Robert's not my boyfriend anymore.'

'No?'

She shook her head firmly. 'We decided to end our relationship. He is too different from me. We don't want the same things out of life.'

Elek was thoughtful for a moment. Then he said, 'I am sorry, Kate.'

'Well, don't be. I'm not sorry. It's over, and I'm happy about that now. Elek, can I ask what changed your mind about selling Hillside House?'

He shrugged. 'I like it here now. It's

different. Strange, perhaps, but I like it. I can stay here, I believe.'

Her heart lifted with his words. She smiled and said, 'Have you any means of making coffee in this ancient mansion of yours?'

'Of course. I have water and a kettle. Everything! I will show you.'

'Then let's have some coffee.'

★   ★   ★

As they sat at the kitchen table drinking Elek's coffee, Kate found herself wondering how long it had been since anyone apart from Elek himself had done this. Ten years, she guessed. Not since Colonel Fenwick passed away. Frances had said he'd probably had a housekeeper, and possibly he had sometimes sat with her over a coffee or a snack. Perhaps he had entertained friends sometimes, too, but not in the kitchen surely? That wouldn't have been the thing at all. People like Colonel Fenwick liked to keep up their traditional standards.

'This old house must be just full of memories, Elek. So many people will have passed through it over the years: the people who built it, and all those who have lived here since — not least Colonel Fenwick, of course. Possibly some of those people will have been famous, as well.'

Elek smiled. 'Many people, and many memories. Yes, I think so. It would be a crime to do what your Robert wants to do.'

'No longer my Robert, Elek,' she said quickly. 'But, yes, I agree with you.'

It was so restful there that evening. The house was warm enough now the season was moving on. Elek was gentle company. The conversation was easy. It seemed a good time for swapping stories.

'Elek, you've never told me how and why you bought Hillside House. What were you thinking at the time?'

'But I did not buy this house,' he said with a smile.

'No?' She frowned. 'I don't understand.'

'It was given to me.'

'Given to you? Who by? What on earth do you mean?'

'It was a gift.'

'From whom?'

He opened his arms wide and said, 'I don't know, Kate. All I know is that it happened.'

She shook her head, perplexed. 'Elek, it doesn't make sense. Nobody gives somebody else a house anonymously. Why would they?'

'I don't know,' he admitted with a disarming shrug. 'But let me explain what I do know.'

20

Elek's story was astonishing. It strained Kate's credulity, but she hung on, fascinated, and heard him out.

A letter had arrived from a solicitor several years earlier, telling him that he had been gifted a property in England by a donor who wished to remain anonymous. The property was located in Northumberland, a part of the United Kingdom of which Elek had never even heard.

He had assumed initially that it was some sort of scam, like the letters that come over the internet from Nigeria advising you that you've inherited a great deal of money and that once the sender knows the details of your bank account the money will be paid into it.

'Also,' Elek said, 'there are the offers that come by email from very wealthy men in Russia who are eager to support your business if only they knew where to send their investment funds.'

'I know, I know!' Kate said, laughing. 'I've been there, had them. And there are the eager benefactors who on their death bed in some mission in the Congo decided to donate all their wealth to me. All they needed me to do was to send them the number of my bank account and the bank's sort code.'

'Did you do it?' Elek asked, grave-faced.

'Oh, yes! That's why I'm still digging soil and moving paving slabs for a living.'

Elek grinned. 'Somebody must send them their bank details. Otherwise, these people on the internet would give up and get a proper job.'

'So you didn't respond to the solicitor's letter, I take it?'

He shook his head. 'I put the first letter in the rubbish bin. The second one I kept. I also kept the other letters that came every few months. But I did nothing about them. I couldn't believe it was true that someone had given me a property in England. But still the letters kept coming from the solicitor in London.'

'How extraordinary,' Kate said, shaking her head. 'And you had no idea who the donor was?'

'None at all. I still don't.'

'So what did you do, Elek?'

'Nothing, nothing at all. It was a difficult time for me. My father had died the previous year, my mother was very ill, and soon to die herself, and my business was in trouble. Every minute I was awake I worked hard. I was approaching exhaustion. So I did nothing about these stupid letters for a couple of years.'

'And then?'

'And then things got worse. My mother passed away. I had no other close relatives. So I was alone. But I didn't care much about that. I was too sad, and too busy trying to salvage my life.

'Then, as I told you once before, my

business collapsed anyway. I lost my land and my house. I had nothing, nearly nothing. And I was exhausted by then. My life was over.'

Kate winced. Elek's story was heart-breaking. So much pain and trouble, and much of it so evident still in his face and voice when he told her about his life.

She reached out to touch his hand. 'Elek, I'm so sorry. You must have had a terrible time.'

He squeezed her hand and smiled that gentle smile that was becoming so familiar to her. 'Thank you, Kate. But please don't be sorry for me. It is not your concern, and besides, I am a happy man now.'

'I hope you are,' she said, wanting to believe that was true.

'Of course I am!' he said, laughing. 'I have this falling-to-bits old house, my rubbish tomatoes in my cold, cold garden. I have my work and my friendship with you, my neighbour. What more could I possibly want?'

She laughed back, and shook her head. 'A big pile of money, perhaps?'

'No, no!' He wagged an admonitory finger at her. 'That is no good. Wanting lots of money is not the way to a happy life. Maybe for your Robert, but not for me. I am Elek Costas. No money, perhaps, but a happy man!'

He finished with an open-armed flourish and a big grin. It was impossible to remain sad for long with Elek Costas. He began to laugh. Kate joined in. She couldn't help it. Their laughter filled the room and drove away the shadows of neglect and misery.

'Oh, Elek!' she said eventually, dabbing with a tissue at her eyes. 'You must stop. It is dangerous to laugh like this.'

'You think so?' he asked, looking worried.

'Not really, no!'

She shook her head, and the laughter started all over again.

★　★　★

'So what happened after your business went down the tubes?' Kate asked eventually. 'You were going to tell me. Then you made me start laughing.'

Elek grinned. 'I am so sorry, Kate.'

'Don't be. Laughter is a good thing. What happened?'

'Well, one day when I had nothing to do any more I remembered about this supposed gift in England. I found the letters about it — I had several letters by then — and I thought about it. I became intrigued. Was it true? Could this be real? Who would have done this?

'I decided to come to England to investigate. I still didn't really believe there was anything here for me, but I wanted to know what was going on. I wanted to know who was behind these letters, and what they wanted from me.'

'What about your family, Elek? Are you married?'

'No wife, and no children. I was never married.'

'No?'

'I was too busy working to have a family of my own. So I was free to please myself. I came to England.'

'And what did you discover?'

'I discovered this wonderful old house. Never had I imagined it would be such a place. Even if the house existed, I was sure it couldn't be anything but a shed or a ruin. But I was wrong. It needs some care and attention, perhaps, but it is still a wonderful house.'

'I agree. You're quite right. I used to get so frustrated with Robert when he refused to see that.'

'Well, not wonderful for everyone, perhaps,' Elek said quietly, 'but it is for me, and perhaps for you too. It took me a little while to get used to the idea that it really was mine. However, I have discovered nothing at all about the person who gave it to me, or why they did so.'

He gave an eloquent shrug to emphasise his sense of mystery.

'I know no more now than when I

was in Cyprus. The lawyer I saw in London said he knew no more himself. He had the keys and he had instructions, but he had no idea who had sent them to him. It was all handled by some very clever person in such a way that he could not know.'

'Some very devious person, as well,' Kate said, shaking her head at the story. 'But perhaps the solicitor did know but wouldn't say?'

'Perhaps,' Elek agreed with an expressive shrug. 'Who knows?'

Kate thought it over and then said, 'I may be able to shed some light on this, Elek. Not a lot, but a little.

'After you arrived, I did some research, because I wanted to know if you really were the new owner of Hillside House. At the time, I couldn't believe it.'

Elek grinned. 'We had a big argument that first day. I remember it well. I was so sorry afterwards. The truth is that I was very nervous and worried — about everything!'

'I understand. I didn't then, but I do now. It must have been very difficult for you. Very stressful, too, coming all this way to such a situation.

'Anyway, what I can tell you is that Hillside House was owned by a Colonel Fenwick until his death some ten years ago. Then it was left to a Mrs Fenwick.'

'His wife? That is normal.'

'Yes, it is. Except that no one knew the colonel was married. He was believed to be a bachelor.'

'No one knew?' Elek looked puzzled. 'How is that possible?'

'I don't know. But I would like to find out.'

'Me, too,' he admitted. 'Do you know who owned the house after Mrs Fenwick?'

'You! Only you, according to the official records in the Land Registry. You appear to have acquired it from Mrs Fenwick. How that happened, I have no idea. Does her name not mean anything to you?'

He shook his head. 'Nothing at all. I

have never heard of the lady, or the colonel either. It is a mystery, but one I came to England to solve.'

'Then let me help you, Elek. I, too, would like to know how all this came about.'

'It's a deal,' Elek said with an appreciative smile. 'You are very welcome.'

21

It was wonderful for Kate to have someone competent and capable to help her. In the past, she had brought in people — usually, but not always, men — from time to time to help, but none of them had been entirely satisfactory. They had enabled her to do things that would have been impossible on her own, but after a day or two she had been glad to see them go.

Some of the older men had made it obvious that they believed she didn't know what she was doing. They had been gardening all their lives, and they knew with utter certainty that you couldn't do this or do that. Mixing herbaceous perennials with vegetables like runner beans was a big no-no, for example. They also knew that doing physical work in the garden was not for females, even though they themselves had such bad backs that they couldn't possibly help with moving paving slabs.

Then there were the young lads who were strong and willing enough but who didn't seem to be prepared to use their initiative or even their common sense. Their tendency was to cover rubbish with soil rather than pick it up and dispose of it properly. Explaining how to protect the roots of plants, especially of trees and shrubs that were being transplanted, was often a waste of time when the person she was instructing was impatient to ram the plant into the ground and get on to the next job.

The women she had taken on occasionally had probably been the worst of the lot. Two girls who were students on vacation and needed to earn a little money to go on holiday with had been excellent. Unfortunately, they had only stayed a fortnight. Otherwise, the women who had helped her had been more hindrance than help. They often knew a lot about flowering plants — certainly with regard to their own likes and dislikes — but usually had been either unwilling or unable to give the help Kate really needed with jobs like moving heavy timbers and digging through heavy clay and surface rock.

Elek, however, was a revelation. He could do anything, and would do it willingly. She soon ceased to marvel at the way he could work continually for several straight hours without pause or break, doing whatever needed to be done. His experience and knowledge soon came to the fore, too. Often he knew more than her, or he could suggest solutions to problems that she hadn't even been aware had arisen. He was a joy to work with.

Now she straightened up and walked to the side of the huge new lawn area they had been preparing for seeding. It was almost ready. Almost, she thought with a frown, as she scanned the ground to see if it was truly level. But something was niggling away at her, something about the central area.

'Elek! Can you spare me a minute?'

He looked over his shoulder at her, and then put down the railway sleeper he was carrying to the raised bed he was building.

'Goodness, Elek! You shouldn't be moving those things on your own. They're far too heavy. You'll do your back in. Give me a shout when you want to move one. I'll help you.'

He shrugged. 'I can manage. What was it you wanted?'

'I'm not sure about this lawn area. I don't want to seed it before we've got it right, and I'm just wondering if it is right. What do you think?'

Elek studied the area for a moment. Then he walked all the way around the edge, scanning it. Finally, he laid on the ground several times and studied it from that angle, too. She looked at him anxiously as he came back towards her.

'There's a slight bump in the middle,' he said.

She grimaced. 'That was what I feared.'

190

'It's where the rock comes close to the surface,' Elek added. 'We'll have to take it out. If we don't, the grass will die off there in dry weather.'

She nodded. He was right. They couldn't ignore it. The soil would be too thin in that area.

'What a nuisance! Just as we were nearly done, and ready to seed it.'

She was tired and exasperated. Removing the topsoil again, and then removing the subsoil to get at the offending rock, was going to take time and strength she felt no longer had left that day. She'd had enough. She just wanted to go home, have a shower, cool off, and have something to eat and something cold to drink.

Now this. It meant they would have to come back tomorrow, and push back the start to their next project. She grimaced. She felt quite despondent.

'Don't worry,' Elek said gently. 'Just leave it to me. I'll soon get it sorted.'

And she did. She was so exhausted and dispirited that she sat and watched

191

Elek make a start. With the topsoil removed, and the sub-soil dug out, he took a heavy crowbar and a hammer and chisel to the offending sandstone.

He tossed the lumps of rock into a wheelbarrow. When it was half-full, Kate roused herself and went to lend a hand. They worked then until late in the evening, side by side until the topsoil was restored. Then Elek began to scatter the lawn seed, working rhythmically and systematically to ensure a good coverage.

Kate sat and watched until the job was done. As she did so, thoughts she had been harbouring for some time returned to the surface of her mind. This time they could not be ignored or sidelined until a better time. This was the time, she decided. There couldn't possibly be a better one. Why wait any longer?

When Elek had finished, he walked over to her. She patted the ground beside her and said, 'Sit down, Elek. Please.'

'I'm OK. I'll just turn the sprinkler on, and then we can go home. Maybe tomorrow morning we can come and check things before we move on to the next project.'

She nodded. 'But sit down now for a moment. I want to talk to you before we leave.'

She knew that Elek hated sitting down before the day was done, but he did so now to accommodate her.

She shook her head and smiled at him. 'I just don't have your durability, Elek. I get tired!'

He smiled back. 'I'm a little older than you, Kate. When you've been gardening as long as me, you'll be just as durable. Tough as old boots, as they say!'

'I doubt it,' she said with a chuckle.

'Seriously, Kate,' Elek added, 'you are a good worker, like me. You would have been very welcome to work alongside my boys in Cyprus.'

'Planting potatoes?' she said with a smile.

'And tomatoes.'

'Them, too, of course. Well, I'm sorry I won't have the opportunity. But that brings me to the subject I wanted to talk about.

'Elek, you've been wonderful these past few weeks. I couldn't have managed without you. I know that for sure. I would be way behind schedule — and even more worn out!'

'We work well together,' Elek said with one of his enigmatic shrugs. 'I am very happy to help. I enjoy this work.'

'Good. I know that. I can see it every day. Elek, would you consider making our arrangement permanent?'

'Permanent?' he asked with a puzzled look.

'Would you consider becoming my partner in the business, instead of just working for me on a casual basis? Together, we can achieve so much more than I can on my own. We've proven that over these past few weeks.

'Besides,' she added, 'I like working with you. I enjoy your company, as well as everything else you contribute. What do you think? Or do you need time to think it over?'

Elek sat in silence for a few moments. Then that familiar smile spread across his face. 'Kate,' he said shyly, 'you do me a great honour. Partners? I would love to continue working with you. I can think of nothing I would like more.'

'Good,' she said, smiling with relief. 'Then that's what we'll do — we'll make the business a partnership.'

'What will we call it?' Elek asked.

Kate laughed. 'Do you know, I haven't even thought about that yet!'

22

Frances said, 'Goodness, dear! Do you think that's wise?'

Kate nodded. 'It is,' she said adamantly. 'I'd been thinking about it for some time. I just didn't know how to broach the subject. Then, the other day, it felt right to ask Elek how he felt. I was a bit nervous, because I thought that if he was uncomfortable with the suggestion, he might disappear on me. I didn't want that.

'Anyway, he was very nice about it. He seemed surprised, and pleased to be asked, which was a relief.'

'I'm sure he was. I'm surprised he didn't grab your hand off!' Frances smiled and added, 'You do seem to lack a bit of self-confidence, don't you?'

'Whatever do you mean, Frances?' Kate asked, a little upset by the comment.

'Well, think about it for a moment. You are a well-qualified young woman who has started her own business at a time when the national economy is doing very badly. For a couple of years you've worked like a Trojan to get your business off the ground — and you've done it!

'You now have more work than you can handle. You worry about clients having to wait for your services. All this, mark you, when so many small businesses are struggling to make ends meet and falling by the wayside because there isn't enough demand for their services. I think you've done extraordinarily well.'

'So?' Kate said with a shrug. 'It's not much of a business, is it? I mean, I'm not exactly making a fortune.'

'Oh, Kate! What are you like? Look here, you're doing really well, young lady. You can afford to be proud of what you've accomplished. For goodness' sake, stop hiding your light under a bushel!'

Kate chuckled. 'Oh, Frances. Really! You do know how to make me feel good about myself. Have I done all that — everything that you've said?'

'Yes, you have,' Frances said firmly. 'And stop being so self-deprecating and modest.'

'You say the nicest things. Robert always thought I was wasting my time. Sometimes I used to be close to believing him.'

'Robert was no good for you, Kate. He didn't understand you, or what you were doing, because you as an independent businesswoman didn't fit very well into his plan for . . . well, for Robert, really. I was going to say for the world, but I think he was more interested in himself than the rest of humanity. You're well rid of him, if you want my opinion.'

Frances went to put the kettle on, the little ritual that always punctuated Kate's visits. Left to her own devices for a couple of minutes, Kate luxuriated in the warm glow that her old friend had created and felt proud of herself.

'So,' Frances said when she returned, 'you decided to invite Elek into the fold. What made you do that, I wonder?'

'Well, as you know, I've been wanting someone to help me for a long time. I just haven't been able to find anyone remotely suitable, until Elek came on the scene.

'We've been working together for a couple of months now, and it's amazing how much we've accomplished together. Elek is absolutely tireless! He works me into the ground, and when I sink with exhaustion he just carries on himself until I insist that he stops and allows us both to go home.

'Not only that, though. He's a very bright man. He's knowledgeable and experienced, and he has his wits about him. If there's a problem I can't solve, Elek usually can. So we're a great team, and I like him a lot. I want him to stick around. Offering him a partnership seemed one way to do it.'

'You probably didn't need to go that far,' Frances said with a smile. 'From what you've just said, I'm sure he enjoys working with you, too. And doesn't he need the money, you were saying?'

Kate nodded. 'I believe he does. I wouldn't say he came here in bare feet and rags, exactly, but he hasn't got the money to do much to renovate Hillside House, which is what he wants to do. That, of course, is what Robert was counting on when he was pressuring Elek to sell to him.'

'There you are, then. You can help each other, can't you?'

Kate nodded. 'I believe we can. In fact, we already do, and not only with the business. I've been helping him work on his own garden, too.'

'At Hillside House?'

'Yes. It's a long-haul project, for our spare time, but we've made some progress.'

'How wonderful,' Frances said, surprisingly. 'Do you think that in time it will be possible to fully restore the garden?'

'I'm sure it will, but it's going to take a year or two. Perhaps longer.'

'That's all right,' Frances said, 'you're both still young enough to do that. Good for you!'

★ ★ ★

A little later, Elek himself arrived to mow the lawn again.

'All the rain we've had,' he complained, 'makes the grass grow.'

'You're telling me!' Frances said. 'Not to mention the weeds.'

Kate just smiled, although she did feel like asking Elek if he never got tired. But it was good that he had befriended Frances, or she him. There was no doubt that she needed help with the garden. Possibly with other things, too.

That would have been another job opportunity for him, she thought: setting up as an odd-job man. That would have gone down well in Callerton. There were a few old dears who would have been glad to pay for his services, just as Frances was presumably doing.

'I must be going,' Kate announced. 'I want to put a load of washing in before I go to bed tonight. I'll see you tomorrow, Elek. Probably you, too, Frances.'

'I'll just walk you to the gate, dear,' Frances announced. 'Elek is doing so much around here; I'm in danger of not getting enough exercise.'

'Is he doing more than cutting the grass?' Kate asked as they stood at the gate.

'Just a few little things,' Frances admitted.

'Like putting up shelves?'

'Yes. That, too. You noticed in the kitchen?'

Kate nodded and smiled. 'He really is a very handy man, isn't he? But don't you go wearing him out. Garden Futures needs him even more than you.'

'Garden Futures? Oh, is that what you're calling the business now?'

'It is. After long and earnest discussions, my partner and I reached agreement on the name just last night.'

'Hmm,' Frances said with a knowing smile, 'I like it!'

23

Before they began work on a new project, Kate and Elek returned to Miss Carrington's cottage for one last look at their handiwork from earlier in the summer, and to take some final photographs for the record. It was early morning. The sun had been shining for several hours already, unhindered by clouds of any description. The bees were hard at work amongst the delphiniums and the lupins, and they were nosing experimentally into the roses as the new petals unfolded.

'It's beautiful,' Elek said quietly, as they stood together looking down the length of the garden. 'We have done a good job for Miss Carrington, I think.'

Kate nodded. It was beautiful. Almost perfect.

'If only there could be tomatoes amongst the flowers,' Elek added, 'and perhaps some potatoes.'

'Oh, Elek!'

She laughed, and suddenly realised she was holding Elek's hand. They stood as they were for a few moments. Then he turned towards her.

She smiled and put her arms around him to give him a brief hug. 'I'm so happy, Elek.'

'I can tell you are,' he assured her. 'And because of that, I am happy also. We've done so well here, the two of us.'

'Thank you, partner!' she whispered.

She pressed her face into his chest. He kissed the top of her head. Surprised, and yet not surprised at all really, she drew back and looked up. Very gently, he kissed her on the lips. She kissed him back, and clung to him.

'I must take some photographs,' she said, breaking away with regret, and wondering what had come over her.

A new voice intruded into the morning air. 'I'm so glad you are both admiring my garden!'

Kate spun round. 'Oh, Miss Carrington! Good morning. I hope we didn't disturb you?'

'Disturb me? I'm sure I was up long before you young things.'

'Good morning, Miss Carrington,' Elek added. 'What a lovely day.'

'Indeed it is, Elek. Were you intending to do anything in particular, might I ask?' she added, turning to Kate.

'I just wanted some early morning photographs, while the light is good, for record purposes.'

Smiling broadly, and managing to give the impression that she didn't believe a word of it, Miss Carrington nodded. 'I'm very pleased with what you've done here,' she said. 'Thank you so much, Kate and Elek.'

'It has been our pleasure,' Elek said gravely. 'And now, Miss Carrington, you have the most beautiful garden in Northumberland.'

'I do believe you are right, Elek. Since you are here, both of you, I wonder if I might ask a question, or make a proposal?'

'Of course,' Kate said. 'What is it?'

'Well, you really have done a lovely job here, making this wonderful garden, but now I am thinking I need someone to help me maintain it. The work will be far too much for me alone, much as I like gardening.

'So it occurred to me to wonder if you might be prepared to retain your involvement here, and undertake some routine maintenance on a contractual basis. Is that something you would be prepared to consider?'

'Why, of course,' Kate said quickly, knowing how useful an arrangement like that would be, particularly over the winter months. It was important to have a secure income stream, however small.

'We would be very happy to make that sort of commitment. Perhaps I can think about what would need doing in detail and send you a sensible proposal, with cost estimates?'

'Perfect,' Miss Carrington said promptly. 'I hoped you might say something like that. Now, if you have a few minutes to spare, can I offer you both a cup of coffee before you go on your way?'

'Absolutely,' Elek said. 'I mean, perfect!'

* * *

It was a time for smiles and laughter, and for Kate confusion that lasted all day long. Busy as they were with the new project, and hard work though the heavy digging on former farmland proved, the early morning was never far from her thoughts.

On the drive back to Callerton she was still wondering what had happened. She had wanted Elek to kiss her. She knew that. And she had wanted to respond, too. So she had, and she had no regrets. But what did it mean? She wasn't sure.

She just hoped she hadn't revealed her feelings too openly. The last thing she wanted was to drive Elek away by being too pushy. She might feel drawn to him, but what did he feel?

Oh, why was life so complicated? Why couldn't she just ask him? It was so silly to carry on like this, but she felt the moment had to be right, and now wasn't the moment.

One thing she was sure of, though, was that the world had become a different place since Elek's arrival. One way or another, he had come to occupy a central place in her life, and she was very glad of it. Working together so much, seeing so much of each other, they had become close almost without realising it was happening. He had crept up on her, or she on him. And now he had kissed her — or she him!

She smiled happily and glanced sideways at him as they drove away from Miss Carrington's cottage, trying to see him in a new and very different light.

'What?' he said, catching her expression.

'What's happened to us, Elek? What happened back there at Miss Carrington's this morning?'

He shrugged and smiled. 'You know as well as me, Kate. Even better, perhaps.'

She pulled into a lay-by and stopped the truck. 'Kiss me again,' she commanded, turning to him. 'Properly this time.'

Elek did so.

When they drew apart, Kate shook her head and smiled happily. She knew now they had both meant it. It had not been an accident or a mistake.

Gazing into her eyes, Elek smiled once again and said softly, 'I didn't see this coming.'

'Nor me,' she admitted.

'Are you happy about it?'

'Very much, Elek. Of course I am. How about you?'

'Me, too.'

'Let's just go home then,' she said, smiling. 'We have a lot to talk about.'

'We also have some work to do,' he pointed out. 'Planning the new project, remember?'

'True,' she said with a reluctant sigh.

'But can we go home afterwards?'

'Absolutely!' Elek said. 'Is that the right thing to say?'

'Absolutely,' she told him happily.

* * *

The remainder of the day dissolved into a dream. They managed to agree a few key points about the next day's work. Then they gave up and returned to Kate's cottage, where they got to know each other better than ever. A celebratory glass of wine was opened, and somehow, despite the wine, a meal appeared on the kitchen table. It had been a lovely day, Kate thought, and now it was fast becoming a wonderful evening.

But there were still some big and difficult questions hovering around them that would not go away, and that would have to be dealt with even more urgently now. Life couldn't all be roses.

'Tomorrow,' Kate said firmly, 'I'm going to make a start on finding out more about Hillside House. We've got to know what's been going on there.'

'Is it possible?'

'I don't know, but let's travel hopefully and see how far we get.'

'But for now?' Elek asked.

'For now,' Kate said dreamily, 'let's just pretend we don't need to know anything more at all, and that we have no more work to do — ever!'

24

Where to start? It was a good question. Kate was taking the day off by arrangement with Elek and their client. Elek was flying solo today, which he was well capable of doing. Kate herself was determined to make progress with her enquiries about Hillside House. She wanted to know who Mrs Fenwick was and how Elek had ended up the current owner. Elek wanted that, too, possibly even more than she did.

But there would be no answers unless she put in some time, and that was what she was going to do. They couldn't go on any longer as they were. Elek needed to know some answers, and so did she.

After breakfast, she made herself a mug of strong coffee and sat down at her computer to give it some logical thought. Where to start?

She decided to begin by taking the simple course of assuming Mrs Fenwick was the colonel's widow, even though no-one in Callerton seemed to think the man had ever been married. After all, local people didn't always know everything, whatever their belief.

As a professional career soldier in the declining days of the British Empire, she knew Colonel Fenwick would have spent a large part of his life well away from Callerton. That would have been inevitable in those days. Not just in bases in Germany either, like more modern soldiers. He could have soldiered in colonies and territories over half the world, and not just in big countries like India. There would have been countless little islands and peninsulas, stand-alone cities like Aden, and all those frontiers that ran between peoples who didn't much like each other. The British Army used to be, and go, almost everywhere.

What all that meant, Kate felt, was that people who had spent their own lives here in Callerton had no idea what a man like Colonel Fenwick might have got up to on his travels and postings. He might well have been married, whatever local opinion held. So she would begin by assuming that he had been, and that Mrs Fenwick was truly his widow. That was the most straight-forward place to start. If she exhausted that possibility, she could explore other options.

She sat at her computer and started punching in questions for Google. Although she knew no details, she had a vague idea that the world of officialdom recorded people's births and deaths. Probably marriages, too, she thought. So that gave her somewhere to begin.

The website of the General Register Office, with its records of births, deaths and marriages, soon appeared on the screen. It was possible, for a small fee, she discovered, to obtain replacement marriage certificates. That gave her hope. If you could replace your marriage certificate, then someone somewhere must keep a record of marriages.

It was also possible, again for a small fee, to discover when a marriage took place, always provided you knew the name of at least one of the partners. Better if you knew the names of both, of course, but that wasn't actually necessary. One would do.

She took a deep breath and edged her chair closer to the screen. Then she hit a snag. You did need to know the approximate date and the place of the wedding. She frowned and grimaced. Date and place? She had no idea. What to do now?

She sat back and thought about what she did know. Colonel Fenwick had died aged seventy-nine, some ten years earlier. She knew that much, at least. Frances had told her.

If he had ever married, she guessed it would most likely have been between the ages of twenty and forty. So that would have been between 1944 and 1964. Approximately? She grimaced.

Very approximately!

It was all a bit fanciful. But at least she had a range of dates now to use for an initial search. However fanciful, that gave her something to do. She got started. Unfortunately, enough John James Fenwicks had been married in England and Wales between 1944 and 1964 to have filled many an entire country on their own. Talk about searching for a needle in a haystack! she reflected with a wry grin.

She needed some way of narrowing the list down. Using the name of a place might help. A county, at least.

Typing in 'Northumberland' did help. It helped a lot to narrow the list down, but nowhere near enough. It would still take half a lifetime to work your way through the list, she thought with a groan — never mind the cost! Anyway, even if the colonel had got married, it needn't have been in Northumberland. It could have been in London — or Penzance or Timbuktu, for that matter!

She needed more information. But where on earth was she to find it? There was nobody to ask. Not that she knew, anyway. Nobody in Callerton even thought Colonel Fenwick had ever been married. And perhaps he hadn't.

It was time to talk to Elek again.

* * *

'Elek, is there anything personal in the house that might have belonged to Colonel Fenwick?'

'Not much.' Elek shrugged. 'Mostly it is just furniture.'

'No clothes?'

'No.'

'Or private papers? Records, or account books even?

'Only reading books. In one room there are many books. That is all.'

Kate thought for a moment, and then said, 'Could we have a look this evening?'

'Of course. What are you thinking?'

She grimaced. This wasa little complicated.

'We want to know who gave you Hillside House, don't we? It must have been this Mrs Fenwick, as she was the previous owner. But who is she, or was she? The colonel's widow, or some other relative? And why did she give you the house?

'To answer those questions, I think we need first to find out who she is, or was — she might not be alive herself now. What I'm doing at the moment is trying to find out if Colonel Fenwick was ever married. If he was, was it to this mysterious lady, Mrs Fenwick?

'That's what I'm working on, but it's difficult to make progress. I need to know more about the colonel himself. Then, perhaps, I'll be able to find him in the official marriage records. And then I might be able to discover something more about Mrs Fenwick. I might even be able to prove that she is the colonel's widow!'

Elek looked totally confused by this complicated explanation. His eyes had glazed over. It was understandable.

'Don't worry, Elek,' Kate said, taking pity on him. 'I know I didn't explain that very well. I tell you what, though. Let's just see if we can find anything more about Colonel Fenwick at the house.'

25

It was clear, Kate soon concluded, that someone had been through Hillside House long ago to remove all personal traces of Colonel Fenwick. His clothes, for example. They were all gone. So, too, were any business and personal papers there might once have been in the room that seemed to have been his study. Goodness knew what had happened to them.

Probably the search and removal had been legally orchestrated by someone: a solicitor, perhaps. It had certainly been thorough. Equally certainly, it had not been undertaken by vandals or thieves. There was no damage anywhere in the house.

Even so, she hoped at first that they might find something that had been overlooked, but as time went by she began to despair. Elek gave up altogether and announced that he would do some work in the garden. She didn't blame him. Their search was looking likely to be fruitless.

Curiously, Colonel Fenwicks's books were still there in the study, a room that could almost be called a library. In dusty rows, they lined the shelves from floor to ceiling on three walls. Why on earth had they alone been left behind? Like everything else, they could easily have been cleared away. Some of them might even have raised a little money.

She was glad they were still there, though. They were the one thing that said anything about the former owner of the house. The titles suggested that many of the books were intended to sustain the memories of a military man in retirement. In fact, many of them seemed to be part of a trail pointing to where Colonel Fenwick had spent a good part of his professional life.

He must have spent much time in the Arab lands, Kate decided, looking at titles about North Africa, the Gulf

States and countries further afield in the Middle East. There were even a few about Cyprus. She wondered idly if Elek had noticed those. But none of the books seemed to help her in her quest. She glanced inside the fly leaves and the front covers, looking to see if any had been given as a gift, especially a wedding gift. It was a forlorn search, and it yielded nothing useful.

Some had a date and a place written in pencil: Aden 1960, Suez 1954, even Casablanca 1973. But it was hard to read anything into those brief inscriptions other than possibly that they were where and when the books had been purchased, or otherwise acquired. A few looked as if they had been found in back-street bazaars, or bought from itinerant booksellers rather than WH Smith or Waterstone's.

The good colonel probably ran out of reading material from time to time, Kate decided wryly. We've all done that, haven't we? There are times when absolutely anything to read is better than nothing at all.

Oh, dear! What else is there? Nothing, absolutely nothing.

★　★　★

She gave up and went outside to join Elek, who was still working in the garden. Her search had petered out, and she couldn't let the entire day slip by unproductively.

'Anything?' Elek asked.

She shook her head. 'Give me those little pruning shears,' she said. 'You can use the long-handled ones, unless you're doing something else?'

'I'm doing something else,' he said with a quick grin.

'Then don't let me stop you! At least one of us needs to do something useful today.'

Elek was actually in the midst of clearing a patch of rough ground. While he used Kate's rotavator, which really was too heavy for her to manage comfortably for long, Kate did some savage pruning on an old climbing rose that had reached mammoth proportions. Undisturbed for such a long time, branches of it had reached twenty feet or even more in length as it cascaded over one of the outhouses. Clearly, something was to its liking in the immediate environment.

The work occupied them for an hour or so. Then they sat with glasses of orange juice on what once had been a lawn, and talked.

'So you found nothing useful in the house?' Elek said.

Kate shook her head with resignation. 'Nothing at all. Everything of a personal nature has been removed — by someone unknown. All that's left, pretty much, are Colonel Fenwick's books.'

'And his pictures.'

She nodded. 'Oh, yes. There are a few pictures on the walls of the study. Landscapes. Nothing of any value, though, I shouldn't think.

'Mind you, just looking at the books

was quite interesting. They seem to say where Colonel Fenwick spent much of his life. The Middle East, mostly.'

'Even Cyprus, I think.'

She nodded. 'Yes. I saw a couple of books with Cyprus in the title.'

'One or two of the framed photographs on the wall are of my country, too.'

'Really?'

'Near Akrotiri,' Elek said with a yawn. 'There's a British military base there. And there's another one at Dhekelia. They were kept after Cyprus became independent, I read once, in order to keep a British presence in the eastern Mediterranean.'

'So Colonel Fenwick probably spent time there?'

'He must have done, if he was ever working in the Middle East.'

'Interesting,' Kate mused thoughtfully.

'Many British soldiers and RAF men have married local women over the years,' Elek added. 'Often they return to

Cyprus to live when they retire. They like the climate, I think.'

'I thought all the immigrants were from Russia?'

'There are many Russians there now, it's true, but always there have been a lot of British people, especially around Paphos.'

The conversation gave Kate something else to consider. Could Colonel Fenwick have been one of those military men who married a local woman? Was that a possibility worth pursuing? Perhaps it was. She certainly didn't have any other avenues to pursue at the moment.

26

It was hot to start with, and somehow the heat just built up even more as the afternoon progressed. So did the dust, as Elek continued rotavating. Clouds of it rose into the air and covered everything within reach.

'Stop!' Kate cried at last. 'Elek, stop!'

He saw her motioning to him and switched the machine off.

'What is it?' he asked.

'Just look at us, Elek!' Kate said, laughing, and spitting out dust. 'Look at the state we're in! We look like coal miners. And it's far too hot now to continue. Let's give it a rest.'

'It's just nice now,' Elek said. 'I feel at home in this temperature.'

'Oh, Elek! You can't be serious. Let's finish for the day. We've done enough. Let's just go to my place, have a shower and get changed. Then we could have something to eat and something cold to drink. How does that sound?'

Elek made an unconvincing show of considering the offer carefully, and with some doubts. 'OK,' he said eventually, with great reluctance. 'If you insist. Do you?'

'You fraud!' she cried, bursting out into laughter. 'You're just as hot as me. You just won't admit it.'

'Come on, then,' Elek said. 'Let's go.'

* * *

It was cool in the cottage. Old stone walls were well able to provide shelter from great heat. Sometimes in winter Kate even wondered if the cottage would ever warm up, but at this time of year, on a day like this, there was nowhere better to be.

After the shower, Kate laid on the sofa and said, 'Elek, tell me what people in Cyprus do to stay cool in hot weather.'

Elek needed no further invitation. He

joined her on the sofa, saying, 'Well, first they find a girl, then they find a quiet corner of the island, then they take out a bottle of ice-cold wine . . . '

'Oh, they take a fridge with them, do they?'

Elek, laughing, admitted, 'I forgot about that part.'

She turned to ruffle his hair. 'Hungry, thirsty?' she asked affectionately.

'A bit,' he admitted.

'Come on, then. Let's see what we can find in the kitchen.'

* * *

Things were so good now, Kate thought happily as she prepared a salad to go with the trout fillets Elek had found in the fridge and now was grilling like a master chef. The two of them made a great team, at work and at home. What a wonderful summer this had turned out to be.

She wouldn't think about the future,

she had already decided. The present was enough. But she had every confidence that there would be a future, and that somehow it would be one that she and Elek shared. Their joint business venture had, if anything, brought them even closer together. The only outstanding problem was the old one about how on earth had Elek come to be here in Callerton. That was still a mystery.

First thing tomorrow, she resolved, she would take up the challenge once again. There would be no peace of mind for either of them until every possibility had been run into the ground. One way or another, they simply had to find out who Mrs Fenwick was, and if it was she who had given Elek the gift of Hillside House.

And now, just this afternoon, Elek had inadvertently given her a couple of new leads to explore.

★　★　★

231

First thing the next morning, she started all over again with her computer and Google. On the off chance, she contacted one of the many commercial websites offering to sell information on births, deaths and marriage records, but that was no good. She didn't get anywhere. It was no different to going through the General Register Office website.

So she came back out, thought again about what Elek had said the day before and then typed into Google 'Marriage' and 'Cyprus'. That search gave her an entirely different group of websites to explore. Some of them really were intriguing. The pace of her search quickened then, her interest growing by the minute.

First there was a lot of general background information to absorb. Civil marriages had been legal in Cyprus since 1923, she learned. That meant that records of them would exist. She guessed that British servicemen marrying on the island would have been more likely to go down that route than through the Orthodox Church, or indeed through one of the mosques serving the Turkish population.

Next she learned that the island had been a British colony prior to independence in 1960, and that in the early 1970s Turkey had invaded and split Cyprus into a Greek part and a Turkish part. Now it was a member state of the European Union. At least, the Greek part of it was. The status of the Turkish part was a little uncertain.

Again, all this was useful background information. It didn't immediately answer any of Kate's questions, but it did suggest that one way or another Cyprus was a country for which records would have been kept of significant events such as marriages.

Even better, she moved on to find an official UK website that dealt with the records of births, deaths and marriages for members of the UK Armed Forces and their families. That really did seem like striking gold.

She paused then, to draw breath and to consider where to go next. She didn't want to rush things now. She felt that she might be on the brink of discovering something important, and she wanted to take her time, and search thoughtfully and thoroughly from now on.

★　★　★

It took her a couple of days, days in which Elek was left to work on his own.

'I can't stop now,' she explained. 'We need answers, and I feel I'm getting close to them.'

Elek smiled and kept out of the way. He didn't mind being left to work alone. She knew that anyway. He was quite capable of doing so. Besides, he knew as well as she did how important to both of them her searches were. They simply had to clear away the uncertainty and confusion over Elek's ownership status at Hillside House.

Then the answer to yet another

online search simply took her breath away. There weren't all that many John James Fenwicks who were members of the British Army and had married in Cyprus in the range of years she examined. And only one of them gave Hillside House, Callerton, Northumberland as his permanent home address.

27

She stared at the screen with astonishment for several minutes, scarcely able to believe her eyes. Then she repeated the search and came up with the same answer. At that point she switched off, held her head in her hands for a few thoughtful moments and then went out to give Elek a hand in the garden once more. She needed some breathing space.

'You've done so well here,' Elek,' she said with approval, hoping she was masking her distracted state.

'Praise, indeed!'

Elek dropped the rake he was using and came to take hold of her. Happily, she clung to him. But she couldn't tell him. Not yet. Right now, she was still guessing. She had to be sure. And for that, she needed more information. But just for the moment she wasn't ready to look for it. She wanted, needed, her insides to settle down a bit.

Not that any of it really mattered, she told herself. All that mattered was Elek. She knew now she loved him, and that he felt the same way about her. Nothing else really mattered. Who cared where he had come from, or why he was here?

All the same, she couldn't put off the completion of her search for ever. She had to know. She had to make sure.

* * *

That evening Kate completed her investigations. She returned to the website she had found most helpful so far and searched the records dealing with births. It was there, the information she had guessed she would find. Her heart pounding, she came away from the computer, switched it off and went outside for some fresh air.

She sat on the little patio facing south and west, and stared out across the valley as the last of the sun's rays lit up the distant hills. She was calm now. It was a good thing Elek was back at his own place for the moment, giving her time and space to think. What she had to do now was work out how she was going to use the information she had sought so eagerly, and finally had found. Working out what would be for the best wasn't going to be easy.

After a little while, she accepted there was no alternative to the straightforward approach. Anything else would just leave questions bubbling and the tension rising until she exploded. She got up, went back inside and rinsed her face with cold water. Then she combed her hair, slipped into a lightweight summer jacket and set off to see Frances.

28

'So what happened, Frances?'

'Hello, dear! You startled me.' Frances straightened up from her roses and turned to face Kate. 'I beg your pardon? Whatever do you mean?'

'You don't have to tell me, of course, but I think you should. We can't go on much longer like we have been doing.'

'Are you quite all right, Kate, dear? You don't seem it. Have you been working too hard? Come on. Let's go inside and sit down.'

Kate followed her elderly friend indoors, trying to remain focussed.

'Now sit down, dear. Please.'

Kate shook her head resolutely and weighed in with the questions she had rehearsed in her head.

'What happened to your marriage to Colonel Fenwick, Frances? And why on earth such secrecy? I thought I was your friend. You should have told me. Then we could have avoided all this running around, and all this . . . all this deceit.'

Frances stared hard for a moment, with not a hint of expression on her face.

'Frances?'

'Would you like some tea?' the older woman said at last. 'Please sit down, Kate. You may as well,' she added, sitting down herself.

'No tea, Frances, thank you. And I don't want to sit down. Just tell me, please, what's been going on.'

Frances sighed and spent a moment collecting her thoughts together. 'Do I gather you have continued ferreting away at things that are not your business?'

At least she wasn't denying it, Kate thought with relief. Despite the unaccustomed sharpness of tone, somehow that made it easier for her.

She sat down at last.

'You know I have, Frances. I've kept

you informed at all stages. I've told you everything, as I discovered it.

'Anyway, I couldn't leave it, especially not now.'

'Not now?'

Kate nodded, but declined to say anything more for the moment. She just waited. Frances was the one who should be answering questions, not her.

Frances sat quite still, her hands clasped together in her lap. She would have made a very good Miss Marple, Kate thought wryly. Almost perfect, in fact. What a cunning little thing she was!

'You obviously believe my life should be an open book?' Frances said.

'Well . . . that's very unfair!' Kate sighed wearily and shook her head. 'Put like that, I suppose I should apologise. I'm sorry, Frances. But, really, you could have told me, and avoided all this.'

Frances shrugged. 'So what have you discovered?'

'That you were married to Colonel

Fenwick, for one thing.'

'And how, might I ask, did you discover that?'

'By searching on the internet. I found a website that has marriage records for members of the British Armed Forces who married abroad.'

'Oh, yes. The wonderful, insidious internet,' Frances said with a sigh. 'Is nothing sacred anymore?'

'Not much, no.'

'I suppose not. So what else do you want to know?'

'Well, obviously, the marriage didn't work out. What happened, if I might ask?'

Frances mulled it over for a moment, and then seemed to decide it was better to say something than simply to deny everything.

'John Fenwick and I did marry, it's perfectly true. We married in Cyprus, where we were both on Her Majesty's Service. John was in the army, and I was otherwise employed. You must forgive me, Kate, but I will not speak of my employment. Let us just say my work required strict confidentiality.'

'You were a spy?' Kate asked with astonishment after a moment's thought.

'I come from a different generation to you, Kate. Like so many women during the war, and for a time afterwards, I vowed never to speak of my work. I never have done, and I never shall.'

Kate was amazed. Yet it seemed so right. This prim and proper little woman . . .

Yet Frances was a redoubtable person. Of that, there had never been any question. It was just that this possibility had never occurred to her. There had never been any reason to suspect it. Frances had given no hint of it whatsoever.

'So what happened?' she said again, in a gentler tone this time. 'If you care to tell me, that is?' she added.

'The marriage was a mistake. We should have known better, and we probably did. But we were young enough to fool ourselves into thinking at the time that it was what we both wanted. Quite soon we discovered our mistake.

'John and I remained fond of each other, but we had to go our separate ways. It is very much easier for people to do that now than it was then, of course. The divorce laws have changed so much. So have the moral rules society lives by. Religions have declined. All of that. People no longer sign up in significant numbers for togetherness until death does them part. But it was different then.

'So it was difficult to take the decision we took. Very much so, and more so for John than for me. The officers' mess could be an unforgiving place in those days. Marriage failure was almost one of the cardinal sins. All the same, we chose to go our separate ways, even though we never divorced.'

'Yet you live here, where he lived?'

'I do. But I came here to live only after John had died.'

'Because?'

Frances shrugged.

'Would it be because he left you Hillside House?'

'Yes, of course,' Frances said with a flash of irritation. 'In part, at least.'

'Yet you bought this cottage?'

'Oh, Hillside House was far too big and grand for me, a woman on her own with a modest lifestyle. So initially I rented this cottage. Later, when I had come to feel settled, I bought it.'

'But kept Hillside House?'

Frances nodded. 'I didn't know what to do with it at first. I just thought that if I took my time, eventually the answer might come to me.'

And it did, Kate thought with grudging admiration. How clever of you, Frances!

'So you stayed here?'

Frances sighed. 'Kate, dear. You are very young. How could you understand? John Fenwick was the love of my life, the only one. I believe I was that for him, too. So, yes, I stayed, even though he was gone.'

They sat in silence for a minute or two then. What a sad tale, Kate thought miserably. What a waste.

Frances seemed drained. The confrontation had perhaps been too much for her. Kate began to feel guilty. All the same, she couldn't let Frances off the hook quite yet. With a wan smile, she said, 'There's more, isn't there?'

'Is there?'

Kate nodded, took a deep breath and plunged on into territory where she was less sure of her ground.

29

'There's Elek, for one thing,' Kate said gently. 'He was — and is — your child. That's why you gave him Hillside House, isn't it?'

Now, for the first time, Frances looked shaken.

'You and your husband had a child, a boy. It's there, Frances, in the official records. He was born a month or two before you were married.'

Frances gave a wan smile. 'You really are a clever little thing, aren't you? So my guilty secret is out?'

'No, it isn't, Frances. I have told no one. Besides, there's no reason to think of the birth of a child as a guilty secret, especially not these days.'

'There was reason enough then, in certain quarters. You haven't told Elek?'

Kate shook her head.

'My guilty secret,' Frances mused wistfully. 'I have wished so often that we had handled things differently, but at the time we did what we both thought was for the best.

'John and I knew by then that we wouldn't stay together. We also knew, with great sadness, that there was no way we could bring up a child to have a normal life. He would just have been parked somewhere, while we got on with our busy and often dangerous lives. There was also a possibility, a real possibility, that our work would one day result in our child becoming an orphan. We didn't want that.'

'So you had him adopted?'

Frances nodded. 'Yes. John's housekeeper and her husband, in Cyprus, were a childless couple, and they were very fine people who wanted and deserved a proper family life. John suggested giving the child to them to bring up as their own. After a certain amount of hesitation, I agreed. We both thought it was for the best.'

'And that was that? You just gave him up?'

'Well, not quite, not altogether. The Costas family were given a substantial sum of money to allow them and our son to have a better life than they could have afforded otherwise. And over the years I kept an eye on the boy from a discreet distance, through intermediaries. But I never interfered. I could see that the Costas were doing an excellent job with our little boy. They were a very loving family, which we were not and never could have been.'

Kate felt even more sad, even though she had anticipated a revelation something like this. It just seemed so cold-hearted. Had there really been no alternative?

Who am I to judge? she thought then. Frances was telling her about a world, and a time, of which she herself knew nothing.

And now? And now Elek's father was long gone, and his mother a little old lady. The causes to which they had dedicated their lives were no longer of much concern to anyone outside a university history department.

'What about now, Frances?'

'Now?'

'You might as well bring the story up to date.'

'Oh, dear! Well, I learned several years ago that the Costas couple, husband and wife, had both passed away, and also that Elek's business was in trouble. That disturbed me. I have to admit that I was very upset.

'But suddenly I knew what to do with Hillside House. So I transferred the ownership to Elek, reasoning that if he sold the property the proceeds would allow him to rescue his business.

'Unfortunately, events moved too quickly. The economic crisis struck Cyprus, and Elek disappeared for a time. I didn't know what had happened to him. Then, amazingly, he arrived here suddenly to claim his inheritance.'

'His gift, you mean.'

'Yes, I suppose I do. It's not really an inheritance, is it?'

'And then you met him for the first time since he was a baby?' Kate said, refusing to be distracted.

'Yes. Yes, I did. For the first time since he was a very young baby I laid eyes on my son. One day, I asked him to mow my lawn, so that I could be close to him.'

Suddenly Frances looked stricken, and close to tears. Kate gasped and leapt up to hug her. She couldn't help it. What was done was done, she thought sadly. There was no going back.

'Oh, Frances!' she gasped. 'I'm so sorry. I've brought all this on you. What have I done?'

Frances shook her head and managed to straighten up in Kate's arms. 'No,' she said. 'It's not your fault, Kate. It's mine, mine and John's. Don't you upset yourself.'

They sat together for a while then, with Kate hugging the older woman and doing her best to comfort her and herself. Somehow they weathered the storm.

★   ★   ★

'What now?' Frances asked eventually.

Kate shook her head. 'I don't know, but you must talk to Elek. It would be wrong not to.'

Frances nodded. 'But he'll go away if I do, won't he? I'll never see him again.'

Nor will I, Kate thought with mounting terror. Oh, Lord! What are we to do?

30

Kate and Frances were still in the same place, still sitting together, when there was a knock at the back door and a cheery call.

Elek! Kate thought, almost with horror. She glanced at Frances, who just shrugged.

'Come in, Elek!' Kate called.

She heard the door opening, and a few moments later Elek came into view. By then, she was getting up, doing her best to smile.

'Hello, Elek,' she said bravely.

'Kate! I didn't know you were here. I have come to cut the grass again. The rain we have had lately . . . '

He broke off and focussed anxiously on Frances. 'Something is wrong?' he asked.

Frances gave a weak smile, but couldn't bring herself to say anything.

Kate was in a quandary. She didn't know what to do, or to say, for the best. She didn't want a distressed elderly lady to be even more upset. On the other hand, there was her loyalty to Elek. She couldn't lie to him, or deceive him. That was unthinkable.

Elek started towards Frances, perhaps fearing that some medical emergency had overtaken her. Kate held him back with one hand. He looked at her even more anxiously.

'Kate, we must do something. Miss Murray is . . . '

She shook her head.

'Elek, I have something to say to you.'

'But, Miss Murray . . . '

'No, Elek! No. Wait.'

He stood still, even more puzzled now.

'Elek, I have found Mrs Fenwick. She is Colonel Fenwick's widow, and she's the person who gifted Hillside House to you.'

Elek's eyes widened with surprise

and, for a moment, delight. Then the look faded, to be replaced by apprehension and suspicion.

'So?' he said. 'What else are you going to tell me?'

Holding on to his arm with one hand, she half-turned towards Frances. 'This is Mrs Fenwick, Elek.'

'You?' he gasped, staring hard at Frances. 'It is you?'

Frances gave a little nod, but a smile was beyond her.

A smile seemed beyond all three of them at that moment. They were all in a state of shock. But Kate couldn't stop there, once started. Something drove her on. Some mad impulse wouldn't allow her to hold back and conceal any of the truth. It was as if she had taken a truth drug, or was being tested by a lie detector. She wanted — she needed — Elek to know everything she knew. Why should she be the only one to know?

'There's something else, Elek,' she said quietly, trying hard to stay calm.

He looked at her with a worried expression.

She glanced at Frances, but there was no help coming from that quarter. It was up to her. She had to do it all herself. Well, why not? It was only fair. She was the one who had conducted this mad campaign. Frances had told her to stop, but would she listen? Not for one moment. She had wanted to know the truth. Now she did, and she was the one who had to tell Elek. No-one else was going to do it.

'Elek, how all this came about . . . I mean, the reason why Mrs Fenwick gifted Hillside House to you — that great mystery we have been desperate to understand! — is that she and Colonel Fenwick are, or were, your natural parents. Frances is your mother, Elek.'

She saw Elek's face whiten with even greater shock as he absorbed what she had just told him.

'No!' he said, almost with panic. 'It can't be true.'

He stared desperately at Kate, as if

wanting to hear her say it was all a joke, that she was teasing him.

'I'm sorry that it's come out like this, Elek. And I'm truly sorry that I'm the one who has had to tell you.'

He stared now at Frances, who met his eyes and gave a tentative nod, confirming what Kate had just told him.

'You knew this?' Elek said, turning back to Kate. 'You knew this all the time? So all those things you were doing, and telling me . . . You just made them up?'

'No, Elek! Of course not. I have only just found out. I was just as shocked as you. I am still. I came here to confront Frances with what I'd discovered. She admitted it. And now, as you can see, she's very upset herself. We're all upset!

'All I can add, Elek, is that your parents had reasons for what they did when you were born. They believed they were giving you a better life than they could give you themselves.'

'They gave me away? You,' he said, addressing Frances now, 'you gave me away?'

Frances seemed to come back to her senses at last. 'We did, Elek. It seemed to be for the best at the time, but over the years I came to regret it bitterly.'

'You gave me away,' he repeated, mumbling to himself now.

Kate wrapped her arms around him. 'Oh, Elek!' she said desperately. 'I'm so sorry it's all come out like this. But it's not the end of the world! At least we know all about Hillside House now. And it doesn't make any difference to us, does it, darling?'

Gently, he eased himself away from her and stepped back. He stared hard at Kate for a moment and shook his head, as if rejecting her and everything he had learned. Then he turned to leave.

'Elek!' Kate cried. 'Please wait.'

But he didn't.

When she followed him outside, she realised he was not going to stop for her, or for anyone else. She called again but he didn't slow down or even glance back.

She collapsed in a heap on the path and began to weep. 'What have I done?' she whispered through the tears. 'Oh, what have I done?'

31

The remainder of the day, and the night that followed, passed Kate by in a daze. She couldn't eat. She couldn't sleep. She couldn't think. She just felt terrible. Elek had disappeared, and it was all her fault. What had she done?

She bitterly regretted ever pursuing the question of how Elek had come into ownership of Hillside House. Why, oh why, had that ever seemed important?

Even more, she regretted what she had told Elek, and the manner in which she had told him. It had just poured out of her, in an unstoppable flood.

She and Frances had both been in a state of shock, and they had passed that on to Elek. He must have been devastated, and now he was gone. She had no idea where he was, and it was all her fault.

The next day there was no sign of Elek. She went over to Hillside House several times, but it was locked up and seemingly uninhabited once again. The whole place just looked incredibly forlorn without Elek. With a sick feeling, she wondered if he would ever return, and even if she would ever see him again. It didn't seem likely. She was sick to her stomach, her head in turmoil.

Then she began to worry if it might be worse than that. Could Elek have been disturbed enough to do something to harm himself? That was an even more terrifying thought. What should she do? Call the police? Have them force an entry into the house?

No. No, she was being hysterical. Elek wouldn't do anything silly, would he? No, of course not. He just didn't want anything more to do with herself or Frances.

It was understandable. He had come

through a lot of trouble in recent years, and now they had plunged him back into a world of uncertainty and upset. Everything he had held dear all his life thrown into confusion. Why would he stay around here for that? He would just have moved on, she suspected. She couldn't blame him. That's what she would probably have done herself in his position.

Not that she could ever be in a position like that! She didn't know anyone stupid enough to make such a hash of things as she had done. Oh, Elek! Please, please come home!

★   ★   ★

Working was out of the question. There was no way she wanted to bother with stupid plants and spades and things. Her clients could forget about that — and about her. She would never darken their doorsteps again. She was done with all that. Her life was over.

I am misery personified, she told

herself with a grim smile. Absolutely worthless and useless. Not a decent, sensible bone in my body — or thought in my head. Why, oh why, did I do it? Why couldn't I just leave things alone?

★　★　★

She tried Elek's phone several times, but it was no good. In the afternoon she returned to Hillside House again, hoping desperately to see Elek hard at work in his garden. He wasn't. The house was still locked up. Elek was not there.

The old banger of a car he had bought for himself with some of the money he had earned had gone. That too? She wondered how far he would get in it before it conked out and he abandoned it. Not far, she suspected. But then what? She didn't like to think of Elek marching alongside a motorway somewhere. It was too dangerous.

He would be all right, she told herself firmly. Just getting that old car to go in the first place had proved that he was a master mechanic, as well as a top horticulturist. If the car broke down, Elek would fix it. Like he could fix most things. She just wished he could fix the situation they had found themselves in here now. Fat chance of that! He was gone for good. She knew that, really. She just didn't like to admit it.

★ ★ ★

Just before six that evening the front doorbell rang. Kate jerked upright, her heart beating fast. Elek? Had he come back, after all?

Full of hope, yet hardly daring to think it, she got off the sofa and ran to the front door.

'Hello, my dear,' Frances said. 'I came to see how you were.'

Kate stared at her with disappointment. 'Oh, Frances. Hello. I'm fine, thank you.'

'May I come in for a few moments?'

She nearly said no, not now. Instead, she opened the door wide and turned away, letting almost the last person in the world she wanted to see follow her into the house.

'You look terrible,' Frances said when they were ensconced in chairs in the living room.

'Thank you, Frances,' Kate said bitterly. 'I needed someone to say that. You've just made my day.'

Frances seemed unperturbed by the comment. 'Have you eaten anything today?' she asked.

'Of course. Haven't you?'

'I have, thank you. I had some soup for lunch. But what have you had to eat?'

'I don't know!' Kate said with a weary wave of her hand. 'Does it matter?'

'You've had nothing at all, if I'm any judge of human nature,' Frances said calmly. 'Am I right?'

'You, a judge of human nature, Frances?' Kate said with a scornful little laugh. 'You're quite possibly even worse than me!'

'Well, I'm hungry again myself now. Why don't I make us something to eat? Some scrambled eggs, perhaps? That usually goes down well when a person is down in the dumps.'

'Whatever makes you think that's what I am?' Kate said half-heartedly. 'I am absolutely fine, thank you very much.'

'I can see that with my own eyes, dear. I bet you haven't done any work today either, have you?'

Kate shook her head.

'It's all my fault, as well,' Frances said with a sigh. 'I'm the one who brought all this down on you. And please believe me, my dear, I am so sorry about that. This unfortunate situation is the last thing I wanted.

'When I arranged for Elek to have Hillside House, I believed I was doing my son some good at long last, and making some sort of amends for the harm I had done to him. Now I just wish I had set fire to the place when John died, and got rid of it altogether. Then neither Elek nor you would have had to suffer.'

It was a cry from the heart and, coming from Frances, so out of character that it touched something in Kate that until that moment she believed had died.

'Oh, Frances! Don't say that,' she cried, coming back to life. 'Please don't worry about me. I'm perfectly fine. Really!'

Frances studied her.

'I admit I have been down,' Kate added, 'but I'll get over it. I'm not a basket case! You just caught me at a bad moment. That's all.'

'Sure?'

'Yes, I'm sure.'

'What about poor Elek, though?'

'I don't honestly know. I haven't seen him all day. It's not too surprising. He had a terrible shock.'

'Has he gone, do you think?' Frances asked, unable to disguise the tremor in her voice. 'Has he gone for good?'

Kate shrugged. 'Maybe. It wouldn't be too surprising if he had. I just hope with all my heart that he hasn't.'

There was no need for Frances to agree to that. They just looked at each other, and each knew what the other was thinking, and hoping.

'Come on, Frances,' Kate said with a sigh after a little while. 'Let's make some of that scrambled egg you were on about.'

32

Later, Kate walked Frances home. It wasn't far; a couple of hundred yards along the lane. It was a warm evening, and the late sunshine had the hills on fire. Kate suspected that when the sun finally went down, an awful lot of midges would come out to play. It was that sort of warm, humid weather they liked so much.

'Just look at the swallows tonight!' Frances exclaimed.

'Yes, they're getting ready for the big feast,' Kate said. 'And we'd better keep our windows closed tonight. Either that or find some mosquito nets.'

'Oh, no thank you! I had enough of sleeping under mosquito nets when I was young. I don't want to start doing that again.'

There it was again, the reference to a life and a way of living that Kate could only imagine. She wondered if mosquito nets had been used in Cyprus. She must ask Elek what he used to do. Then she remembered that she couldn't. Not anymore.

She and Frances were both very subdued. In their time together that evening, they had begun to recover from the anguish of the past twenty-four hours, but they needed more time to complete the process. If they ever did, Kate thought sadly. Would they? Would she?

Would she ever get over losing Elek? She didn't think she would. Life would go on, of course. She was sensible enough to know that. But she would never forgive herself for losing Elek. She knew that even now.

'Are you coming in, dear?' Frances asked when they reached her gate.

Kate sighed and shook her head. 'I don't think so, Frances, thank you. Not tonight.'

Frances nodded. Then she stood hesitantly, as if unable to decide whether to go in herself.

'The midges will get you out here!' Kate said, nudging her with a little smile.

'I'm sure you're right.'

Still, Frances hesitated.

'What is it?' Kate asked. 'Is anything wrong — I mean, apart from the obvious.'

Frances shook her head. Then she said, 'Do come inside for a little while, Kate. I don't feel like being on my own all evening. I'm so sad after what has happened. You must be, too?'

Kate nodded. 'Go on, then. I'll follow you. Let's have a mug of hot chocolate. That's guaranteed to make us feel a little better.'

Smiling with relief, Frances led the way along the garden path, taking care when she came to the places where the concrete had crumbled. 'I'll have to get this path repaired before the winter comes,' she said over her shoulder.

'Yes. It needs doing, doesn't it?' Kate said absently.

'It was the salt last winter that did the damage, you know. You need to salt the path when it's icy, but that stuff just eats into concrete.'

'Really?' Kate said, pausing and sniffing the air.

'What is it, dear?' Frances asked as she fished in her pocket for the door key.

Kate shook her head. 'Nothing,' she said.

Then she looked at the lawns on either side of the path. 'When was the grass last cut?' she asked.

Frances shrugged. 'About a week ago.'

'It hasn't grown much, has it, despite the warm, wet weather we've been having.'

'I don't know, I'm sure. Come on inside, dear.'

Kate took a last speculative look at the lawns and followed Frances indoors. She felt a slight prickling of hope. Perhaps all was not lost, after all?

★　★　★

Frances seemed really tired now. Kate began to feel a little worried about her. She hoped all she needed was a little rest, and persuaded her to sit down while she made the hot chocolate. She didn't feel very good herself. Recent events had taken their toll on both of them.

'Hot chocolate is a good pick-me-up,' Frances said with a chuckle as she took delivery of the mug Kate had prepared.

'Indeed it is,' Kate agreed.

'Sometimes,' Frances confided, 'especially on a cold winter's day, I brace my hot chocolate with a teaspoon or two of liquid heat.'

'What on earth is that?' Kate asked, puzzled.

'You see that little cupboard over there?'

Kate looked over her shoulder. 'Where you keep the torch and candles for when we have a power cut?'

Frances nodded. 'That's where I keep the liquid heat, too. Would you mind fetching it for me?'

Still puzzled, Kate opened the door of the little pine cupboard attached to the kitchen wall. She peered inside. Then she laughed.

'Is this what you mean?' she asked, taking out a miniature bottle of rum.

'That's it! Now find me a teaspoon as well, if you please. Let's fortify the hot chocolate — and ourselves.'

'It's not winter yet, Frances.'

'No, but we still need a bit of fortifying, don't we?'

Kate smiled agreement and brought a teaspoon for Frances to administer the liquid heat into their mugs of hot chocolate. She did feel a little better now. Frances's company had helped. So, too, had the scent of new-cut grass in Frances's front garden.

★ ★ ★

Suddenly the back door opened. In came Elek, wearing a smile and looking calm and relaxed.

Kate gasped with shock.

Frances gave a little cry. Kate spun round and grabbed the mug of hot chocolate from her before it spilled all over the carpet.

'Ladies!' Elek said. 'How are you this evening?'

'Would you like to join us with some hot chocolate, Elek?' Kate asked, trying to keep her voice steady, trying to match Elek's calmness with calm of her own. 'You must be tired after all that grass-cutting.'

'Thank you, Kate. I would love some hot chocolate.'

She began to heat some milk. Then she couldn't stand it any longer. She took the pan off the hob and spun round.

'Elek . . . ' she began fearfully.

He shook his head and smiled. Then he crossed the room, gave her a quick hug and turned to bend down to kiss Frances on the cheek.

Kate stared for a moment, astonished. Then she turned back to the pan and the hob. When the milk was hot enough, she mixed in some hot chocolate powder. As an afterthought, she also poured and mixed in two teaspoons' worth of rum from the little bottle.

'What's that?' Elek demanded, his voice full of suspicion.

'Firewater,' Kate said hastily. 'I mean liquid heat. It's what we're both having.'

'Oh, that's all right then,' Elek said with a knowing grin. 'As long as it's something healthy.'

'Oh, it is!' Frances said, cheering up.

'Is it all right, Elek?' Kate asked fearfully. 'Have you thought things through?'

He nodded and smiled. 'Yes, it is. It was a big shock at first, but you've given me answers to some of the questions I have had in my head since I was a little boy.

'It's all right for me, Kate,' he added cheerfully. 'Is it for you, too?'

'Of course.'

She moved close and he wrapped his

arms around her and kissed the top of her head. Thank God! she thought, closing her eyes with relief.

'As for you, Mother,' Elek added, moving gently away from Kate and going over to Frances, 'I am so happy to meet you at last!'

He leant down and kissed her tenderly on the cheek. Frances beamed with astonishment and delight, and looked as if she were about to burst into floods of tears.

'I feel like I have come home at last,' Elek added. 'I loved the parents I grew up with — who were good people, and who were wonderful to me — and I love them still. I always will. But here is where I know I should be now — with the two of you.'

'Both of us?' Frances said faintly, clutching his hand.

'Yes, of course. Both of you. Did Kate not tell you we are to marry, and live here and restore Hillside House to its former glory?'

'No, she didn't,' Frances said. 'She

never said a word about any of that.'

'Kate, oh Kate!' Elek said, wagging an admonitory finger at her and laughing.

Kate just stared at him with shock, for the moment rendered speechless. Then shock gave way to delight when she realised he meant it, every word of it.

'Elek,' she said archly, 'is there a proposal of marriage somewhere in there, or have you forgotten that part?'

'Indeed there is. Didn't I tell you?'

'Tell me? You haven't even asked me yet!'

He slapped his hand to his forehead. 'My memory! So what do you say, Kate?'

She laughed and wrapped her arms around him. 'Yes,' she said happily. 'Oh, yes!'

Then Elek kissed her properly, even though they had an audience who was giving them all of her attention.

'How wonderful!' Frances whispered, scarcely able to believe what was happening in front of her.

'Isn't it?' Kate said, breaking away from Elek and reaching down to give Frances a hug.

'And do you know what?' Kate added. 'I've finally worked out who that enormous sweater you've been knitting is for.'

Smiling happily, Frances picked up her knitting and said, 'It's finished now. Elek, would you like to try it on, please?'

We do hope that you have enjoyed reading this large print book.

Did you know that all of our titles are available for purchase?

We publish a wide range of high quality large print books including:
Romances, Mysteries, Classics
General Fiction
Non Fiction and Westerns

Special interest titles available in large print are:
The Little Oxford Dictionary
Music Book, Song Book
Hymn Book, Service Book

Also available from us courtesy of Oxford University Press:
Young Readers' Dictionary
(large print edition)
Young Readers' Thesaurus
(large print edition)

For further information or a free brochure, please contact us at:
Ulverscroft Large Print Books Ltd.,
The Green, Bradgate Road, Anstey,
Leicester, LE7 7FU, England.
Tel: (00 44) 0116 236 4325
Fax: (00 44) 0116 234 0205

THE SURGEON'S MISTAKE

Chrissie Loveday

Matti Harper has been in love with Ian Faulkner since their school days. He is now an eminent cardiac surgeon, she his theatre nurse. Ian has finally fallen in love — the trouble is, it's with Matti's flatmate Lori! But whilst a heartbroken Matti prepares to be their bridesmaid, Lori is being suspiciously flirtatious with another man. How can Matti tell Ian without appearing to be jealous? Best man Sam Grayling tries to help, but only succeeds in sending things from bad to worse . . .